*The monstrous dog came to a stop in front of me, drops of water falling off of his long tongue as he panted heavily. His big brown eyes stared into mine with such force, they caused me to freeze in place. Was he trying to convey a message? I wanted to run but was afraid he would follow me. With a dog this size chasing me, I wouldn't stand a chance.*

*Off in the distance, an unfamiliar man appeared. I guessed him to be a slave. He called off the dog, who relaxed at once, then rolled over and offered his belly for a rub.*

Prudence Willard
April 3, 1862

## SECRETS OF WAYFARERS INN

*Family Secrets*
*River of Life*
*All that Remains*
*Greater than Gold*
*A Flame in the Night*
*Never the Twain Shall Meet*
*The Innkeepers' Conundrum*
*At Face Value*
*Moonlit Shadows*
*Picture This*
*Forget-Me-Nots*
*All the Inn's a Stage*
*Stolen Goodbyes*
*Red, White, and True*
*The Secret Ingredient*
*Submerged Surprises*
*Hushed October*
*Before It's Too Late*
*Mercy's Song*
*There's No Place Like Holmes*
*A Place to Belong*
*Crossing the River*
*Who Let the Dogs Out?*

SECRETS OF
WAYFARERS INN

# *Who Let the Dogs Out?*

JANICE THOMPSON

**Guideposts**

New York

Secrets of Wayfarers Inn is a trademark of Guideposts.

Published by Guideposts Books & Inspirational Media
100 Reserve Road, Suite E200
Danbury, CT 06810-5212
Guideposts.org

Cover and interior design by Müllerhaus
Cover illustration by Bob Kayganich, represented by Deborah Wolfe, LTD.
Typeset by Aptara, Inc.

Printed and bound in the United States of America
10 9 8 7 6 5 4 3 2 1

# *Who Let the Dogs Out?*

*In loving memory of Daisy Mae and Gigi,*
*two of the gentlest pups to ever nose*
*their way into my heart.*

*The righteous care for the needs of their animals,*
*but the kindest acts of the wicked are cruel.*
Proverbs 12:10 NIV

# CHAPTER ONE

"Gigi! Here, girl! Gigi, where are you?"

Tess looked up from her spot at the register as the inn's most recent guest, Geneva Matthews, entered the lobby, leash in hand.

"You've lost your dog?" Tess asked as she glanced the woman's way. "Again?"

Geneva nodded and swept her loose red hair over her shoulder. "Yes. I was about to dress her in the most adorable little plaid skirt to match mine." She pointed at her red, black, and white plaid outfit. "But she slipped away, that little doll. Sometimes I think she's part Houdini and part dachshund."

Tess wouldn't argue with that. The past twenty-four hours had proven the feisty little dachsie was quick on her feet. And boy, could that hound bark. Tess had never heard so much noise come out of one little canine.

Before she could say a word, a flash of red shot across the carpet as the miniature dachshund blazed across the living room and up the stairs.

"There you are, baby girl!" Geneva's words elevated in pitch as she sprinted after her pup. "Slow down! Mommy needs to get you dressed! We want to wow those judges at the party tonight! You never get a second chance to make a first impression, you know!"

Too late, at least as far as Tess was concerned.

The hyper young woman bounded up the stairs behind her dog and disappeared from view. Tess did her best not to sigh out loud as the words *"Good riddance!"* flitted through her mind. Just as quickly, she scolded herself. Geneva and Gigi were guests at Wayfarers Inn and deserved as much kindness as any other guest, hyper or not.

Still... Tess pondered the current state of affairs at the inn. Whose idea was all of this again? Oh, right. LuAnn's. She walked into the office where LuAnn was hard at work on the computer then plopped down into the chair across the desk from her friend.

"Whatcha doin' over there, LuAnn? Planning for your big day?"

LuAnn glanced her way. "Oh, sorry. I guess I should be working."

"Are you kidding me? If I were you I'd be picking out flowers and looking at bridesmaids dresses and choosing decor for my reception."

"Okay, I'll admit it, that's exactly what I was doing." LuAnn grinned and turned the monitor in Tess's direction. "What do you think of peonies? Aren't they gorgeous? And I was thinking of a really soft pink for bridesmaid dresses. Nothing over-the-top." She pushed the screen away. "I'm a dreamer. Always have been. It's been hard to let go of the plans I made all those years. But at my age, who needs all the frills? I'm just so blessed to be getting such a wonderful man. I would stand in a field in overalls and T-shirt and marry him, if it came right down to it."

"Goodness. Let's hope it doesn't come to that. Go ahead and simplify your plans, but don't go that far."

LuAnn laughed. "I was just kidding, silly. I still want it to be pretty, and I'm sure it can be, even on a tight budget."

"Well, sure."

"Did you need me for something?" LuAnn asked.

"Nah. I'm just struggling with this whole dog thing."

"Dog thing?" LuAnn looked confused.

"I still can't believe you talked us into opening the inn to pets while the dog show is in town."

"Oh, *that* dog thing." LuAnn pivoted in her chair to face Tess. Her face brightened as she smiled. "Personally, I think it was a brilliant idea."

"If Geneva's little dog Gigi is any indication of what's to come, we're going to have to hire carpet cleaners. And don't even get me started on how Winnie is doing with all of this. You saw what happened at breakfast this morning. She walked out of the kitchen with a tray of blueberry scones in her hand and Gigi jumped her."

"Yes, I saw." LuAnn pursed her lips. "It was good of Winnie to start over and make new ones. She's been a real trouper."

"Yes, but I think you missed the part where Geneva blamed Winnie when her dog took a nibble from one of the scones that had fallen on the floor. Can you believe that? Something about sugar not being good for dogs, especially on competition week."

"Well, it's not good for any of us, if we're being completely honest, but I get her point. Look, I know it's a lot to deal with, but please don't fret, Tess. It's just for a week. Things will return back to normal soon. And let's keep things in perspective. Sure, Winnie lost a tray of scones, but it's not the end of the world."

"True, but I don't think it's fair to expect so much—of any of us."

"I'm sorry." LuAnn offered a sympathetic look. "Maybe it was too much for me to think this would go well. But just know my heart was in the right place. I love the inn and would never deliberately do anything to sabotage any of us."

"Right. Of course." Tess decided to calm herself. No doubt LuAnn really was just trying to help. "Well, anyway, I'll be glad when this week is over. So far only one of the competitors has arrived, and I'm already feeling frazzled. Not sure how I'll handle even more canines. That's all."

"I heard from the Lawson family just now." LuAnn's expression brightened. "They're on the way, but running a little behind schedule. Their car broke down on the way in from Tennessee. But they'll be here by four thirty with their dog, Jelly."

"Jelly?" Tess crossed her arms at her chest. "Interesting name for a dog."

"Technically, I think the dog's name is Angelica, but they call her Jelly for short. I heard Mr. Lawson in the background yelling the dog's name several times while we were on the phone."

"Oh boy. I hope that's not a sign."

"I'm sure it's not." LuAnn laughed. "Sometimes I forget that not everyone loves dogs as much as I do."

Tess thought through her answer before responding. "I love Huck. You know that. I'm just wondering if we bit off more than we can chew by offering to take so many at one time."

For a moment, LuAnn looked worried. Just as quickly, the wrinkles between her eyes eased themselves out. With the wave of a hand, LuAnn appeared to dismiss any concerns. "It's just a test to see if we can take pets in the future. This week will answer that question for us. And look on the bright side—the local paper is doing an article about our temporary change in policy. And guess what? They're tying the story to the historical tale of the inn's most famous canine."

"Wait...we have a famous canine? You mean Huck?"

LuAnn clucked her tongue, as if scolding Tess. "Tess, I thought I was the one who was preoccupied. Did you miss the memo about the Civil War dog that I sent you? It was a really big deal and is a great bit of information we can share with guests who want to know more about our history. I sent you an email with a link to several online articles."

Tess shrugged. "Sorry. I saw something come through about the Civil War, but I don't think I read it in its entirety."

"I wish you had. It's quite the story. You'll have to take the time later on."

"When things slow down. Can you give me the *Reader's Digest* version?"

"Sure. Jack, a mastiff, was a Civil War mascot. He defected from the Confederacy. He switched to the Union side."

"I wish I'd been a fly on the wall during that meeting." Tess couldn't help but laugh. "Pretty sure I've never seen a dog switch sides in a battle before."

"You'll have to read the article. But anyway, he was completely faithful to the men in the 103rd Division. They trained him to understand bugle calls and everything."

"I think we might need the help of the 103rd Division with a certain dachshund. Do you think they're available?"

"Tess, pay attention. Jack was also taught to search for his fallen comrades on the battlefield. Not only that, he kept their morale up. There's nothing like the love of a dog to put a smile on your face."

"I guess."

"I can't believe you're not more excited about this discovery." LuAnn clasped her hands together. "I got such a kick out of it. So did Reena Newberry. You know what a history buff she is."

"Reena Newberry?" Tess let the name roll around in her memory. "The elderly woman who came to stay with us months back? The one whose great-grandmother had ties to the inn? Something about a wedding ring in a loaf of bread?"

"Yes, the one Winnie went to stay with a few months back, remember?"

"Sure. What about her?"

"I sent her a copy of the story about the mastiff. I knew she would enjoy it." LuAnn paused. "Wait…didn't I tell you Reena was coming back to the inn?"

"No." Tess shook her head. "I'm sure Winnie is tickled pink to see her again."

"Oh, she is. She can hardly wait."

"Has Reena entered that yappy little chiweenie of hers into the dog show?"

"No." LuAnn chuckled at that idea. "Beauvine was a rescue, as you might recall. He's definitely not a purebred, so he can't compete. Reena is coming back to Marietta to meet up with the folks from Paws on Wheels. From what I understand, she's one of their main contributors and wanted to be here when they handed off their rescue dogs to new owners."

"Paws on Wheels? What's that?"

"It's a rescue organization that brings dogs up from southern states when the shelters are overcrowded. Ask her about it, and she'll talk your ear off. She'll be here tomorrow morning."

Before Tess could give it further thought, Janice popped her head in the door way. "Tess, we've got a new guest, an older man with a schnauzer."

"That would be Richard Townsen," LuAnn explained. "He's going to be staying in Woodsmoke and Pine."

"Right next to Geneva and Gigi, who are in Sunshine and Daisies. There's going to be a lot of yapping going on." Tess could only imagine how loud things would get in those two rooms.

"Could one of you take care of him?" Janice glanced at her watch. "The café is full, and we're a server short today because Taylor can't be here. I need to help out."

"Sure," Tess said. "And I'll pitch in to help in the café after I check Mr. Townsen in."

Janice nodded. "Thanks. I would've jumped in sooner, but I just got off the phone with Stuart. He and Zelda are up to their eyeballs in wedding plans. You might offer to help Winnie in the kitchen. She's having trouble with the *pup-cakes*."

"Pup-cakes?"

"Yes, cupcakes that look like puppies. Don't ask." Janice disappeared from view.

Tess walked into the lobby where she found their incoming guest seated by the register.

She gave the elderly man a closer look as he reached down to grab his dog's leash. From this angle, his nearly bald head garnered the most attention. Soft brown age spots added a speckled effect to the perfectly aligned creases on his forehead. Tiny wisps of white hair started at the top of his head and partially covered the back but she could see through them to his scalp underneath.

He looked up and smiled. As he did, the most glorious crinkles formed along the edges of both eyes. This was a man who spent a lot of time smiling, no doubt about that. Joy had left permanent marks. His soft white mustache and beard reminded her of her grandfather, and for a moment Tess lost herself to childhood memories. She finally snapped to attention and remembered her manners.

"Welcome to Wayfarers Inn." She offered him a nod and he stood, albeit slowly.

"Takes me longer to do that than it used to." The gentleman's dazzling smile lit the room. "But Schmaltzy and I are happy to finally get here." He gestured to the most adorable black and white schnauzer curled up on the floor at his feet. "That drive up from Lexington took a bit longer than I thought it would. I don't mind admitting, I get a little turned around these days. And that fool GPS thing tried to take me to Marietta, Georgia, not Marietta, Ohio."

"That happens a lot. But I'm glad you made it, Mr...." Why couldn't she remember the name? LuAnn just said it aloud, for Pete's sake.

"Townsen. Richard Townsen. And this little boy right here is Schmaltzy."

"Yes, you already..." She didn't finish the sentence. No point in embarrassing him.

"Well, lookee there!" Richard pointed to Huck, the inn's canine-in-residence, as he moseyed into the room. Schmaltzy walked over and sniffed Huck, who greeted him with a wagging tail. "These two are going to be fast friends."

"Sometimes you can just tell right away," Tess agreed. "Huck's pretty easygoing."

"If I lived in such a wonderful place I'd be pretty easygoing too." Richard looked around the room, and his eyes widened when he saw the crowd in the café. "This place has to be at least a hundred years old, if it's a day."

"Oh, you'll have to read our brochure." She picked one up and passed it to him. "The inn is much older than that. And we have a rich history that ties back to the Civil War. I hope you enjoy learning about it."

"I will. I'm a great history buff." He paused and then sneezed a couple of times. "Excuse me. Allergies."

"No problem." Tess grabbed the tissue box from the coffee table and passed it his way.

He dabbed at his nose and then set the box down. "I've researched the Townsen family all the way back to the 1500s. We're British, of course. We even have our own coat of arms."

"Fascinating. I've been researching as well. Just did my DNA, in fact."

"Me too! It confirmed what I already knew. What about yours?"

"I haven't received the results yet," Tess explained. "But I'm mesmerized by all I'm learning about my ancestors through that ancestry site. Sometimes I lose all track of time when I'm on there."

"There's much to learn, isn't there?" Richard paused and then chuckled. "Though, truth be told, Schmaltzy's pedigree is slightly more impressive than mine. Most of my people were common laborers."

"Nothing wrong with that."

"Nothing, indeed."

She finished the check-in process and led Richard to Woodsmoke and Pine on the third floor. Then Tess checked in on Winnie and Janice in the kitchen. They were hard at work on the most adorable cupcakes Tess had ever seen. Sure enough, they looked just like little puppies. Tess could hardly believe Winnie's handiwork.

"You've outdone yourself," she exclaimed.

"Between you and me, I prefer the cupcake version to the real thing." Winnie gave the cupcakes a pensive look. "But I'm up to the task, regardless. I thought Reena would get a kick out of them. Can you believe she's coming back?"

"I just heard. It's so exciting." Tess turned her attention to Janice, who looked a little distracted. "You okay over there?"

"Yes, sorry." Janice looked up and swiped at her hair with the back of her hand. "My mind is on Stuart's wedding plans."

"How are things coming?" Tess asked. She knew that Janice had been preoccupied of late with the plans for her son's big day.

"They're coming." Janice opened the piping bag and refilled it with icing, then dove into a lengthy story about her incoming daughter-in-law's choice in wedding flowers. She finally paused for breath. "Tess, do me a favor. If I get too caught up in my son's plans, remind me that I should also be helping LuAnn prep for her big day. I don't want her to feel left out."

"I'm sure she doesn't."

"I hope not." Janice lit back into a story about Stuart, something about invitations. When she finally brought the conversation to an end, Tess decided to head back to the café to check on their guests. The place was abuzz with activity. Many of the locals had come by, but a few unfamiliar faces caught Tess's attention as well. She did her best to help serve, then headed up to her room to grab some Tylenol for the headache that began to nag at her.

Sometime around four thirty the front door of the inn opened, and a little boy rushed inside chasing a gorgeous black-and-white cocker spaniel.

"Jelly! Jelly!" The boy shot across the room in hot pursuit. He finally caught up with the pooch, who jumped onto the sofa and nuzzled into the pillows.

A woman with long platinum hair entered with an adorable little girl at her side. She had a pink blanket with dog bones on it slung over her arm. "I'm so sorry!" The woman rushed over to the sofa to fetch the pup as her son did a somersault over the back of the couch. "Jelly's been in the car for hours. She's a bundle of energy right now and just needs to get it out of her system. She's really a very good girl, I promise. You should see her in the ring. Such an angel." The blanket fell to the floor.

Tess couldn't think of anything to say in response so she just nodded.

Huck must have picked up on the fact that another dog had entered the inn. He rushed into the room, took one look at the cocker spaniel, and his tail started wagging.

"Please don't fret," the woman said. "We keep her on a leash. She just happened to jump out of the car and then she took off running before we could grab her."

The dog jumped out of the woman's arms and gave chase around the parlor. The little girl took off after her, and the little boy followed closely behind them, all of them squealing and laughing. The woman managed to catch the pup again and cuddled her in her arms. "I'm Tandi Lawson. These are my children, Callie and Wyatt. My husband, Andy, is parking the car. I'm sorry we're a little later than we'd planned."

"No worries. We're glad to have you." Tess picked up the blanket and smiled as she saw how cute it was. As she handed it back to the woman, she said, "This is adorable."

"Thanks. I bought it from one of the vendors at the last competition." Perhaps she thought Jelly would be calm by now, because she set the pup on the floor. Of course, the spaniel darted around the room.

Andy Lawson entered the room and gave the dog a firm look. The minute the dog saw him, her ears perked up.

"What's going on in here?" Mr. Lawson asked.

"Jelly decided to turn the inn into her own personal playground." Tandi's attention shifted from her husband to Tess. "And I was just trying to apologize for her behavior."

"Angelica, sit." Andy's words were firm but loving. The dog stopped running at once and sat at attention, her tail wagging. "Good girl. Stay."

At least this one seemed to respond to her owner's voice. There was something to be said for that. Tess got busy checking the family in, then she handed them the keys to the Honeymoon Suite on the second floor.

"We hope you'll be comfortable in this space," Tess said. "Our honeymoon suite is oversized with plenty of room for the kids. It should be perfect for a family of four."

"Thank you for thinking of that."

"You're welcome." Tess glanced down at the register and then back up. "And by the way, we're only going to have one other guest on the second floor, a sweet elderly woman who should be arriving tomorrow. You'll love her and her little dog, Beauvine, as well."

"Wonderful. Is Beauvine competing?"

"No." Tess shook her head. "He's not a purebred. Just an ordinary little dog who needed a happy home."

Tandi beamed. "Well, I'm sure he'll make a fine neighbor for our little Jelly Bean. And if there's anything we love, it's dogs."

She couldn't have timed her statement any better. Tess looked over as Geneva entered the room with Gigi, who took one look at Jelly and went into a barking fit. Her high-pitched yaps were enough to cause LuAnn to come racing out of the office.

"Everything okay out here?"

Tess went a bit bug-eyed as the two dogs went to town with their mutual yap-fest. When they finally came to a stop, she turned to LuAnn and said, "Whew! Everything's under control."

The Lawsons headed to the elevator with their bags and disappeared from sight. Geneva's expression tightened as she approached Tess. "I wish I'd known that Jelly and fam were going to be staying here. I would have opted for different lodging."

"Really? Why is that?"

The creases around her eyes deepened. "I don't expect you to understand, since you don't have a dog in the circuit. But it always seems to come down to Angelica."

"What do you mean?"

Geneva looked around, as if to make sure no one else was listening. "I'm just saying, for two years running now, Jelly has taken the Best in Breed prize in the sporting group. Then she moves up the line to Best in Show and takes that too. Two.

Years. Running. She's up against some stiff competition but somehow manages to win every time."

"What are you saying? Do you think there's some sort of cheating going on?"

Geneva shrugged. "Well, I wouldn't go that far. I mean, my little dumplin' does well every year too. Last year she won Best in the hound dog group, and this year, well, we have very high hopes once again. But even if she wins her group, what's the point in moving up when the final round is rigged?"

Tess hardly knew what to say in response. This whole conversation felt awkward and uncomfortable. Not that Geneva seemed to notice. She just kept going, getting more animated.

"This morning I was hanging out with a guy who writes articles for the *Canine Companion* and told him all about it. I hope he'll write a story about it if Jelly wins again. But what if it backfires on me? I mean, I can almost see the story now: 'Bitter Competitor Voices Complaint When Her Dog Doesn't Win.'"

"Yeah, I suppose that's possible. He might slant the story in the wrong direction."

"Probably. And that might ruin Gigi's chances in years to come." Her expression brightened. "Or maybe Jelly will retire after this season. Stranger things have happened."

"I guess." Tess shrugged.

"I know a lot of us would be happy if she disappeared off the circuit." The young woman leaned in close. "Between us," she whispered, "I don't even know how that hyper little spaniel wins her own group."

"Oh?"

"I mean, if you could see the other sporting dogs, you'd totally understand. There's a gorgeous Irish setter who's really got the goods. And we're supposed to believe that Jelly *always* manages to beat her out?" She shook her head. "Anyway, don't take my word for it. There are plenty of other dog owners who would tell you the same thing. I can almost guarantee you, Jelly's going to take the prize this year too. And when she does...well...just watch out. That's all I'm saying. Because something's gonna blow."

# CHAPTER TWO

Tess awoke early Wednesday morning to the sound of barking. She groaned and rolled over in the bed, but the high-pitched yapping coming from the third floor was more than she could take. The little yappers just didn't quit, did they?

Tess pulled the pillow over her head to drown out the noise, but it didn't do any good. How would she ever last the rest of this week until the dog show was behind them? She muttered the words, "Five more days, five more days" to herself, but they were little consolation with her eardrums under assault from the floors below.

When the barking didn't stop, Tess decided to go ahead and get out of bed. A quick shower drowned out the noise below for a few precious moments, and she was able to gather her thoughts. The first rounds of the competition kicked off this morning, so all their guests would be at the arena all day anyway. It would be wonderful to be able to hear herself think again.

She met up with Janice coming out of her room a few minutes later. Her poor friend looked exhausted, if the dark rings under her eyes were any indication. Oh dear.

"You heard it too?" Janice covered a yawn with her hand.

"Heard it? I think the people three counties over heard all of that barking." Tess rubbed her ears. "Remind me to invest in earplugs if this keeps up."

Janice took a few steps toward the stairs. "I just hope our other guests don't complain."

"Well, they're all dog owners too, so hopefully they won't. And maybe it wasn't just Gigi and Schmaltzy. Maybe it was all of them, singing in chorus."

Janice laughed as she headed down the stairs. "Well, that was some chorus, that's all I have to say. It definitely wasn't an angel choir."

"No, it wasn't."

Minutes later they joined Winnie in the kitchen. She fussed and fumed as she flipped pancakes on an electric griddle while tending to the bacon sizzling atop Big Red in a skillet.

LuAnn joined them in the kitchen and reached for an apron to help. She paused and looked at Winnie who muttered under her breath. "Everything okay over there, Winnie?"

Winnie turned to look at them. "If you must know, it's not. I no sooner got out of my car this morning when that little red maniac attacked me."

Tess felt her breath catch in her throat. "Wait...you were attacked by one of the dogs?"

Winnie flipped a pancake and shrugged. "Well, not attacked, really. But she wouldn't stop barking at me. So I closed the door of my car and just sat there until that woman took her back inside." Winnie began the process of stacking pancakes on a platter. "How long until they leave, again?"

"Geneva and Gigi are scheduled to stay through Sunday morning," LuAnn explained. "And don't forget, they'll be gone most of the time. The competition starts today, and Gigi's round is in the afternoon, I think. I pulled up the schedule online because I'm hoping to spend some time there myself. I want to watch our guests in action. I hope that's okay with everyone. Brad is already up there."

"Brad?" This news puzzled Tess. "At a dog show?"

LuAnn nodded. "Yes, his agency is one of the sponsors this year. There's a big banner in the center ring with the Grimes Realty name on it. It's great promotion for his agency."

"Ah, I see." Tess paused to think it through, realizing just how beneficial this could be for local businesses like his. "Is he taking pictures with the winners?"

"Hmm." A thoughtful look came over LuAnn. "Not that I know of, but maybe that's not such a bad idea."

"I'm just happy they're all leaving." Winnie paused from her work to lift both hands into the air in celebratory style. In the process she lost control of her spatula, which flew across the room.

Tess quickly fetched her another while Janice walked over to pick up the one that had landed under a chair at the kitchen table. "This is slightly off the subject, but what is Geneva wearing today?"

"Well, she's all decked out in green," Winnie said. "Tweed."

"Tweed? In April?"

Winnie nodded. "Yes. It reminds me of an outfit my mom wore in the '50s, if you want the truth of it. That skirt is to-the-knee, and the jacket looks like something Jackie O would've worn." She whistled. "And just wait till you see her shoes."

"Let me guess—Gigi is wearing green today too."

"Not just any green." Winnie quirked a brow.

"Tweed." They spoke the word in unison.

"At least it's better than the little berets they were wearing last night when they came in from that party they attended. All of that red and black and white." Tess did her best not to roll her eyes. "If I wanted to visit France, I wouldn't take Huck with me."

"I think it's cute," LuAnn countered. "Maybe we should give some thought to dressing Huck up from time to time."

"In a tweed suit and beret?" Tess couldn't imagine such a thing.

"Well, maybe not that."

Thank goodness the topic changed, and before long they were serving their guests a hearty breakfast. Most of them were in a hurry. Well, all but Richard Townsen, whose dog didn't compete until the late afternoon.

As soon as breakfast was over, the Lawsons and Geneva hurried to their respective rooms to grab the pups and then head to the arena. The next few hours were spent waiting on customers in the café and then prepping for lunch guests. Right before they opened for business again, a familiar woman walked through the front door. Tess couldn't help but smile when she saw Reena Newberry. She was decked out in a pink-and-lime-green floral ensemble that would put a runway model to shame. Every white hair was in place, and her makeup was impeccable, if you didn't count the fact that the eyeshadow was a bit darker on one side than the other. In her arms, she held her little rescue dog, Beauvine.

"Reena! It's so good to see you. How have you been?"

Reena set Beauvine down then clasped her hands together and beamed. As she did, the fine lines on her cheeks deepened, and her thin white brows elevated. "I'm as fit as a fiddle and so is Beauvine, thank you for asking."

"LuAnn tells me you're working with some sort of rescue organization these days."

The tiny crinkles around the elderly woman's eyes grew more pronounced as she smiled. "Oh, yes, Paws on Wheels. They've just arrived at the arena parking lot this morning with a vehicle full of babies who were in high-kill shelters in the Houston area. I've been helping the head of the organization find homes for them all. We've located adopters for the pups, and they will come tomorrow morning to pick them up. It's going to be quite the to-do."

"What a worthy cause, and how sweet of you to help out."

"How could I not? Those poor sweet babies can't help it if they're not purebreds." She picked Beauvine back up, nuzzled him, and planted tiny kisses on his little head. "But then, who-ever said you had to be a pedigree breed to have any value?" Reena paused and wrinkled her nose. "Other than my father, I mean. But he was such a snob." She giggled. "Anyway, I'm happy to be back. Wayfarers Inn holds such happy memories for me."

"It does?"

"Well, of course. This is where I found my little Beauvine and where I met all of you wonderful ladies. And I learned so much about my family's history here." She extended her hand. "I'm still wearing my great-grandmother's ring. Remember?"

"Oh, yes. It was transported north in a loaf of bread. How wonderful, to have such a rich family history."

"I just love to research my family tree," Reena said.

"We have another guest who's into genealogy study. I'll have to introduce you. Richard Townsen is his name."

"Townsen. British. I like him already." Reena rubbed her tummy. "Wayfarers is also the place where I met Winnie." She looked around the room, as if expecting her to materialize. "Is she here today?"

"Yes, and chomping at the bit to see you too."

"Perfect." Reena sighed. "I've missed her so much. I don't mind admitting that I also came back for Winnie's amazing sweets. The last time I was here, she was competing in that big baking competition. Do you remember?"

"How could I forget? She's still the best in Ohio."

"The best across the East Coast," Reena said. "And I should know. I've traveled a lot in my seventy-plus years. I can hardly wait to have more of her snickerdoodles."

"Well, we're glad to have you back. Do you need help bringing in your bags?"

"No, thank you. My driver will do that. He's also bringing in Beauvine's crate."

Sure enough, a man who looked to be in his early forties entered with several bags in tow. Reena introduced him as James, and then Tess passed off the key to Maple and Mum. He returned a few minutes later empty-handed, then went out to his car for more. This time he entered with an empty dog crate in hand. Beauvine took one look at it and started wailing.

"No, don't cry, baby boy," Reena said. "It's not that bad, and you know it."

Indeed, it was not. Tess wasn't sure she'd ever seen such a fancy crate.

James headed back upstairs, and Tess turned her attention to her guest. "Reena, are you hungry?"

"Am I ever! But just let me crate Beauvine in my room and wash my hands. Then I'll join you in the café."

"I'll go up with you and show you to your room. Maple and Mum is on the second floor, the closest room to the elevator."

"Sounds lovely."

Tess led the way to the elevator and chatted with her guest all the way to the second floor. When they arrived, she took a couple of steps toward Maple and Mum and found James putting the dog crate near the bed.

"The café will be open for lunch soon," Tess said. "So be sure to come down for some of Winnie's chicken salad. It's divine."

"I remember from last time. So yummy. And she was so sweet to make some for me when she came to stay with me for a few days a couple of months back. Oh, we had such a wonderful visit."

"We heard all about it. She came back to the inn with marvelous stories about your home."

"Thank you. I so loved having her." Reena paused. "Please ask her to come out to the café to say hello if she has a moment."

"Of course."

"Speaking of the café, I've invited my young friend Jordan Sellers to have lunch with me today. Paws on Wheels is his organization, you see, and we have much to discuss." Reena walked into the room and gasped. "Oh, what a lovely space! Even prettier than the last one." She carried on about the decor, then finally snapped to attention. "I'd better freshen up, but I'll be down in a jiff."

James said his goodbyes, and Reena disappeared into her room. Less than fifteen minutes later she came down the elevator to the lobby, without her canine companion. Just as Reena settled in at her favorite table in the café, Winnie came out of the kitchen to greet her. The two hugged and chatted for a few moments until Reena's guest arrived. Jordan Sellers seemed like a personable young man. He had a laid-back appearance with his curly hair and beard. Tess liked him at once.

She seated the thirty-something next to Reena at the table closest to the window. Reena insisted Tess join them. She agreed, but only for a few minutes. Really, with so much to be done, she couldn't spare a lot of time.

"So, you're from Texas?" Tess asked Jordan as he reached for his menu.

Jordan nodded. "Yes, from the Houston area. We have an overflow of dogs in our shelters, in part due to all of the flooding. You wouldn't believe how many dogs we transported north after Hurricane Harvey."

"You weren't able to find their rightful owners? I'm sure they were devastated."

"When the owners microchip their dogs, they're often reunited, but you'd be surprised how many people haven't gone to the trouble to do that. The strays are held at a shelter for a certain number of days, but then they've got to be re-homed. Otherwise, far too many are euthanized." This led to a lengthy monologue about people who didn't properly care for their dogs. Jordan finally paused and smiled. "Sorry about that. As you can see, I'm very passionate about the subject."

Reena looked up from her menu. "I would be too, if I had to transport as many lost dogs north as you have. I think what you do at Paws on Wheels is admirable." She turned to face Tess. "I'm a big supporter—financially and otherwise."

"And we're happy to have you on board." He gave her a warm smile then turned to face Tess. "We're hosting an adoption event tomorrow morning. Our bus is loaded down with dogs ready for new homes."

"Yes, Reena told me. It's all so exciting."

"We're happy to be here."

"Speaking of being happy to be here, I'm helping Jordan make a documentary." Reena beamed with obvious pride. "I'm going to be in it."

"She's being modest," Jordan explained. "Reena is funding the documentary, which we hope to post online to draw attention to our work. She's given us a tremendous gift by making this possible. It's been a dream of mine for years to produce a movie about our work."

"That sounds wonderful." Tess turned her attention to Reena. "I'm sure you'll do a great job."

"Oh, I hope so. We want to share the news of what Paws on Wheels is doing so others will lend their support. That's why we've set up a booth inside the dog show. Can we count on you for a monthly donation, Tess?"

Reena gave Tess a pleading look, and before she could help herself, she nodded.

"Oh, I knew you ladies would help!" Reena nearly dropped her menu, she got so excited. "Make sure the others know, will you?"

"Oh, I—"

Thank goodness Robin interrupted them. She took their orders, and Tess excused herself to get back to work.

Just as Tess was refilling Reena's and Jordan's coffees for dessert, LuAnn rushed into the café and walked their way. She greeted their guests then turned her attention to Tess. "I just had a call from Brad. He's at the arena and wanted me to know that the Lawson's dog, Jelly—Angelica—just won her breed's division. She's up for Best in Show on Saturday morning at eleven."

"Oh? She won her division?"

"Yes. She did beautifully. From what Brad said, she's a real doll in the ring. Well, he didn't say 'doll' exactly, but you get the idea." LuAnn pulled out her phone and opened a photo. "Check out this picture he sent. I hardly recognize her now that she's been groomed. She's absolutely darling. Every hair in place." LuAnn patted her own hair and laughed. "I should be so lucky."

"Hey, if you paid what those owners pay for groomers you could have hair like that too," Jordan interrupted. "Those competitors pay a fortune just to train and groom their dogs."

"If you think grooming is expensive, you should see the competition fees." Reena pushed her chair back from the table. "It's crazy. That's why I stick with my little rescue pup these days. No purebreds for me." Her eyes took on a faraway look. "Unless the good Lord decides to send me a husband. Then I'll definitely check his pedigree. You can count on it."

Jordan chuckled and then rose.

"I would like to go upstairs and get Beauvine," Reena said. "Then we can finish our visit in the parlor, Jordan, if that's all right with you."

"Of course."

She headed to the elevator, and Jordan settled onto the sofa. Tess continued to make the rounds with the coffee carafe. A few minutes later the elevator dinged, and Reena and Beauvine emerged, followed by Mr. Townsen and Schmaltzy. Goodness, but didn't Richard Townsen look fine in his white suit? And wasn't that bow tie something?

Schmaltzy and Beauvine started the usual dog-sniffing. Tess watched them to make sure they wouldn't end up in a scuffle but found herself more interested in the interaction between Richard and Reena. The older woman blushed as the southern gentleman carried on about how cute he thought Beauvine was.

"Are you headed to the arena for Schmaltzy's first round, Richard?" Tess asked when she finally managed to get a word in edgewise.

"Yes." Richard leaned over and scooped up the little fluff ball, then scratched him behind his ears. "I wouldn't say he's a real contender, but this little fella already knows he's a winner in my book. I don't place much stock in these competitions, if you want the truth of it."

"Then why enter them?" These words, which sounded a bit curt, came from Jordan, who rose from the sofa and joined them. "I mean, if you really don't care about the outcome, why buy a pedigree dog from a breeder in the first place, and why bother to enter the competition at all?"

"Oh, I, well…" Richard scratched his head. "Hadn't really thought about it. It's just something fun to do to occupy my time. And Schmaltzy loves it."

"Does he?" Jordan crossed his arms. "He loves being put on display and paraded around in circles?"

"Well, when you put it like that…"

"The truth is, these pedigree dog shows might be fun for the owners, and they're definitely a way to keep the breeders in business. But I think we all know that the dogs aren't really having the time of their lives."

"I beg to differ." Richard pulled Schmaltzy close. "You haven't seen this fella in the ring. He shows off like a contestant in a beauty pageant."

The two men got into a bit of a back-and-forth argument. For a moment, Tess thought it might not end well. Then Reena rested her hand on Jordan's arm and cleared her throat. "Now, Jordan, let's not ruin a perfectly good visit. Give this precious baby a close look." She reached over and scratched Schmaltzy on the top of the head. "He's absolutely adorable. And just because he's a pedigree doesn't mean he's not as special as the rest of them."

Jordan released a sigh. "Sorry about that, folks. I'm just passionate about the 'Adopt, don't shop' motto."

"If it makes you feel any better, I did rescue Schmaltzy from a tough situation," Richard said. "He belonged to my best friend, who passed away from cancer a year ago. Poor little guy had nowhere to go. Chuck was already training Schmaltzy to compete, so I just picked up where he left off. Somewhere along the way I fell in love with this little fella." A hint of tears glistened in Richard's eyes. "Anyway, he keeps me company, and I don't get a lot of that these days, what with the kids and grandkids living so far away. So competing gets me back out in the world, among people, something I've desperately needed."

Jordan opened his mouth as if he might say something. Just as quickly, he closed it. "Guess I should probably go now, actually. I hate to leave Missy alone with that many dogs. Reena, why don't you come with me, and we'll visit in the car on our way."

She beamed as she said, "I would love that."

Minutes later the crowd dispersed, and Tess found herself in the kitchen, helping with dishes. Winnie was still a bit testy, but LuAnn was bubbly.

"Hey, now that the lunch crowd is gone, why don't we go over to the arena and check out the dog show. I know Brad would be tickled to see us."

"You really want to?"

"Sure. He said there are vendors from all over the country. And maybe we'll get to see Gigi and some of the others compete."

Tess reluctantly agreed when Janice offered to stay behind and look after things. She and LuAnn walked out to the car and then hit the road for the arena. As LuAnn drove, Tess pondered the conversation between Jordan and Richard. Jordan was certainly passionate about his cause, wasn't he? Thank goodness Richard had taken the man's words in stride.

They arrived at the arena in short order, and Tess was stunned to see so many cars in the parking lot. It took some time to find parking, but they finally managed. As they approached the door, she noticed the Paws on Wheels bus to her right, parked in a cleared area.

"LuAnn, check it out." She pointed to the bus.

"Oh, wow. Nice vehicle for a rescue organization." LuAnn's brow furrowed. "Which brings up a question. Why do you suppose Reena and that fellow from Paws on Wheels are so opposed to purebreds?"

"I don't think it's purebreds, per se, they have a problem with. More likely they're worked up about irresponsible breeders. And some folks are of the opinion that breeding is only adding to the problem of overpopulation, what with so many dogs in shelters."

"I guess." LuAnn took a few steps toward the ticket booth. "But there's got to be a middle ground, right? I mean, I love a mixed breed as much as the next person, but there is something pretty sweet about seeing all of those purebreds prance around the ring. I love watching the Westminster Dog Show, don't you?"

"Yes, but please don't say that too loudly around Jordan, okay?"

LuAnn laughed. "I won't, I promise. But like I said, there's got to be some way to make all the dog lovers happy."

"One would think."

After paying for tickets, Tess and LuAnn entered the arena to a bustling crowd of both people and dogs.

"Wow, and I thought Geneva took the dog-thing seriously. Check that out!" Tess pointed to a miniature dachshund dressed up to look like a hot dog.

LuAnn shook her head as she pointed at a vendor's booth advertising high-end dog foods and treats. "Did you see the price on that small bag of food? Forty-nine dollars! Who spends nearly fifty dollars on a little bag of dog food?"

"Someone with expensive taste."

They continued to walk from booth to booth, looking at everything from dog toys to clothes to treats. When they reached the final aisle, the competition area came into view.

"Oh, look! There's Gigi!" Tess pointed, and they stopped to watch as the little prissy thing walked in a circle inside the arena. "Looks like she does know how to behave, after all." She and Geneva looked pretty cute in their matching green tweed outfits, Tess had to admit. Clearly, the judge was smitten too. She took her time looking over the dog before moving on to the next dachshund in the group, a black-and-tan beauty with a very handsome owner.

"Oh, and look!" LuAnn pointed at the banner with the words GRIMES REALTY. "Doesn't that look nice?"

"Sure does. And I'm sure it's going to do wonders for Brad's agency, since the Best in Show round will be televised."

They continued to watch for the next several minutes until the winners were announced. When Gigi's name was called as the best in her group, Tess could hardly believe it.

"Wow!" She glanced LuAnn's way, mesmerized. "Maybe I misjudged the little thing."

"Could be. She really shows off, doesn't she?"

"Mm-hmm."

Geneva accepted the trophy with a broad smile and waved as the other contestants cheered Gigi on. Then she left the ring and disappeared into the crowd.

Off in the distance Tess caught a glimpse of Brad sitting with his aunts, Irene and Thelma Bickerton. LuAnn waved until she caught their attention. Before long they were all together, chatting about what they'd just witnessed. Tess explained that Geneva and Gigi were their guests at the inn.

"So, we have stars in our midst!" Thelma seemed tickled by this notion.

"I wish we could have met them," Irene added. "But she buzzed right past us."

"I'm sure she has a lot on her plate," Tess explained.

They continued to visit with Brad and his aunts. The ladies just couldn't get enough of the dogs and their owners.

Just about the time Tess realized they needed to head back to the inn, a familiar man pressed his way through the crowd and came to a stop in front of them. Andy Lawson looked wide-eyed and even a bit frantic.

"Is everything okay?" Tess asked.

He shook his head. "No. Have you seen Jelly?"

She shook her head. "No, I haven't seen her." She shot a glance at LuAnn and Brad, who both shrugged. "But then again, we've been watching the dachshunds compete."

"She was crated in the family lounge right next to the grooming area. My wife and kids were resting and visiting with friends nearby. Tandi turned to talk to one of the other competitors, and when she turned back Jelly was gone from the crate." Andy couldn't seem to collect his thoughts. "I don't have any idea how she got the lock undone, but you know how she likes to run. I was hoping she would stop if she saw a familiar face. You know?"

"I haven't seen her, I promise."

He plopped down on a seat nearby and dropped his head into his hands. Tess could barely make out his words as he said, "I don't know what to think. Our little Jelly Bean has gone missing."

## CHAPTER THREE

*April 3, 1862*

Prudence hefted the mop bucket to the clearing behind her house. She tipped it over, and the thick, black water poured out onto the parched ground below. This was the driest April she could ever remember. Usually springtime showers caused the clearing to come alive with life but not this year. Only tiny buds of green peeked through the dry ground. They gave her hope that spring would soon be on its way.

As she dumped the water, something in the distance caught her eye. Prudence nearly lost her breath as shadows moved behind a row of sycamore trees in the distance.

"Who goes there?" she called out.

No response came.

Likely her imagination was working overtime. She lifted the empty bucket and straightened up to go back to the well. Before she could turn that direction, the shadows in the sycamore trees seemed to move again. Her heart leapt to her throat. "Wh-who goes there? Make thyself known."

Before she could say another word, a large dog lumbered toward her. She'd never seen such a big one, nor did the breed seem familiar. The enormous mastiff had an oversized head and massive paws. Except for a patch of white on his breast and one on each paw, he was as black as coal. So were his ears, which hung loose and floppy as he sprang toward her.

Her breath caught in her throat as he raced toward her. The words, "No, no, no!" were all she could manage. If he jumped her, she wouldn't be able to stand. The beast was huge.

Before she could think to speak, a whistle rang out, followed by the words, "Down, Jack!"

At once, the dog stopped running and sat down. Prudence's heart *thump-thump-thumped* as she froze in place. Her gaze shifted from the dog, now lying on its back, to the large man in a torn blue shirt who appeared in front of her.

"I apologize for the dog, ma'am." The man's dark skin glistened under the afternoon sun as he took several quick steps in the dog's direction. "I sure didn't mean for him to frighten you. He scared my wife the first time she met him a couple of days back. But this fella's heart is in the right place, that's sure and certain."

"Is he thine?" Prudence set the bucket down and brushed her hands on her apron.

"No, ma'am. We stumbled across him on our journey north. His master is wounded, and the dog wouldn't leave him."

"His master?" Prudence looked around but saw no one.

"Yes'm. He's a Union soldier in charge of the dog's care. But now he's in bad shape, so I'd say the dog is caring for the master. Poor fella took a musket shot to the shoulder a few days back in a skirmish in Virginia. Least ways, that's what he told us when we happened upon him night before last on our way here." The man paused and gave Prudence a pensive look. "We're hopin' you can help him. And us too. We heard there's some folks here who help people like us."

She followed the man through the thicket, beyond the clump of trees, to a small clearing, where she located a family of travelers and a wounded soldier. He was dressed in full Union attire, right down to the sack coat and forage cap, and appeared to be in bad shape.

"This is the dog's owner?" she asked.

The man sighed. "Well, that's a bit of a story. This here fella's from the 103rd Division. He's been put in charge of the dog's care as far north as Philadelphia, and we're along for the ride. The dog's real owner done passed away some time back. Now, if you please, ma'am, we're mighty hungry and in need of sleep. And I'm sure Jack would love a bite to eat and a rest too. Can you help us?"

Prudence's thoughts tumbled around in her head as she tried to decide what to do. The people, she could help. That mighty beast of a dog? Someone else would have to help him. Just looking at him made her knees knock.

The monster rose and took a couple of steps in her direction. His large brown eyes seemed to beg for assistance. So she did the only thing that made sense in the moment. She knelt down and patted the fella between the ears. In return, he licked her on the cheek. She wiped the moisture with the back of her hand and fought the temptation to groan aloud.

The man who'd led her here extended his hand. "I'm Abram, ma'am. Pleased to meet you."

"Welcome, Abram." She turned her attention to the young woman and children. They looked exhausted.

"This here's my wife, Phoebe, and our little 'uns, Clara and Elijah." A little boy peeked his head out from around the woman's leg and grinned a toothless grin.

She offered them a welcoming smile.

"We made it this far with the poor man, and then he couldn't go no farther. So we waited here in the clearing till you came into view."

"I don't know this man. But if it's a stop on thy journey thee is looking for thee has come to the right place."

"Yes'm. We're lookin' for a good night's sleep and some food. These little 'uns are mighty hungry. And then we need help knowing where to go next."

"We're not safe out here. Now, do as I tell thee. Go along that clearing to the farthest edge of the trees, to the bank of the river. Wait for me there behind the bushes. I will come as soon as this man is tended to and lead thee to a place where thee can rest."

"Thank you, miss."

"It is my pleasure. When we get thee safe and settled, I will bring water and coffee. Then, if thy stomachs can bear the wait, I will come a short while later with a thick beef stew."

"Oh, miss. Those words are music to my ears." Abram glanced down at the soldier. "But what do I do with him?"

"Leave him here with me. My husband and I will care for him in our home."

"He would want the dog to stay with him."

She glanced at the mongrel and sighed. "All right. I will figure out what to do with the dog shortly. Right now thee just head on into the woods and do as I say. Before long, I will see thee safely inside."

# CHAPTER FOUR

D o you think Jelly is really missing?" Tess asked. "Maybe she just snuck out of the crate and is running around the arena, having an adventure."

"I hope so, but I doubt that's the case." Andy Lawson lifted his hands, and she could see the exasperation in his eyes. "There's been a lot of jealousy from other dog owners where Jelly is concerned, you see. It's kind of a long story."

"Are you saying you think she's been kidnapped?" LuAnn's eyes narrowed to slits. "Surely not."

"I wouldn't put it past one of the competitors to try to take her out of the race." He looked dead serious as these words were spoken.

A little chill ran down Tess's spine. She couldn't help but think of the earlier conversation she'd had with Geneva. Was this just a coincidence that Jelly had gone missing after winning her division?

"Maybe the crate just wasn't shut right." She looked to her right and then her left but couldn't see past the throng of people. They pressed in on every side. She turned her attention back to Andy, who looked overwhelmed. Poor guy. "She probably managed to get the door open. But we'll help you look for her, Andy. Don't you worry now. We'll find your Jelly."

He nodded. "Just to be safe, I'm going to talk to security."

"Good idea. I'm sure they're very vigilant in a situation like this."

"One would hope. Just do me a favor." Andy leaned in close and lowered his voice. "If some journalist asks you about me, try to distract him. He just about drove me crazy earlier this morning, asking question after question about Jelly."

"Why would he do that?" LuAnn asked.

"For some article he's writing. I thought I'd never shake the guy. If he figures out that Jelly's missing he'll never leave me alone. I don't have time for that right now."

"What does he look like?" Tess asked.

"Early fifties. Salt-and-pepper hair. He's wearing a gray suit and a light blue tie. You can't miss him. He's carrying around a recording device so he can interview people. He's been a real nuisance today. I don't have time to give you the backstory, but there's a reason I don't want to talk to him about Jelly. His articles have done a lot of damage to people in the past."

"Okay, got it." Tess nodded. "What's his name?"

"Winston James. The *Canine Companion* used to run a lot of his articles, back in the day. I don't think they buy his pieces anymore."

"That's interesting. I wonder why."

"I could speculate, but I don't have time. Anyway, he's always looking for news, so I can't even imagine what he'd do if he caught wind of a missing dog story."

"If I see him, I'll point him in a different direction," Tess assured him.

They spent the next several minutes searching every competitor's circle and then every aisle in the vendor's area. Tess alerted every person she could so others would be on the lookout, including Brad and good friend Maybelline Rector. Before long, many of the guests and competitors were taking the search seriously.

Looking past the vendors' booths, Tess spotted a familiar young man. "Isn't that Jordan Sellers, the man who had lunch with Reena this afternoon?"

LuAnn shrugged. "I don't know. I only caught a glimpse of the back of his head just now, but Jordan did have curly hair like that. There are hundreds of people in here, you know."

"I'm pretty sure that was him. I thought he wasn't a fan of pedigreed dogs."

"Well, he is parked just outside the arena, so he didn't have far to come." LuAnn paused and then snapped her fingers. "Oh, I know. Didn't Reena say that Paws on Wheels had a booth in the vendors' area? If so, that explains why he's inside."

"You're probably right."

"Not that it's any of our business. Let's keep looking for Jelly. Eye on the prize, and all that."

"Right." Tess tagged along behind LuAnn and did her best to help, but there was no sign of Angelica anywhere. Before long, they found themselves in the dog grooming area, which butted up to the family lounge. The place was filled with dogs of every kind, some in crates, but many on top of stainless steel tables, where the groomers did their work.

"Will you look at that?" Tess pointed to a curly-haired white dog in the process of being groomed. "My goodness, they're really giving her a pretty hairdo. What kind of dog is that?"

"I'm thinking Maltese. They have that distinctive pure-white coat."

Tess paused and watched the groomer—a young man with dirty blond hair and overly tanned skin—at work. His hands moved with great speed as he clipped away at the dog's hair. Her eyes could barely keep up with his movements.

"I'm mesmerized by that groomer," she said after a couple of minutes watching him at work. "He's fast, but he seems confident in his work."

"Swagger," LuAnn responded. "That's what I'd call it, anyway. He's got swagger."

"Yes." Tess paused and gave him a closer look. "He's really good at grooming, isn't he? I mean, I don't even get that kind of treatment when I go to the hair salon. You would think that dog was worth a million bucks."

A woman to Tess's right must have overheard their conversation. She turned to face them. "She might be, if she wins Best in Show, which is a real possibility. At least, we're hopeful. But trust me when I say that a grooming from Russ Schumer doesn't come cheap, and you have to get on his waiting list months in advance."

"Months?" That seemed a bit extreme to Tess.

"Yes. He's the best in the business." The woman carried on for a few minutes about her dog's possibilities in the ring and then headed off to pay Russ Schumer for his work.

LuAnn faced Tess, eyes wide. "I guess I just never thought about how much money goes into all of this, did you?"

"No."

"And I'm kind of mesmerized by how many people are willing to pay these groomers such exorbitant fees." LuAnn pointed around the room, which was filled with crates. "People take this thing very seriously."

"Which explains why that freelance writer is following after the Lawson family." Tess paused to think it through. "He's in it for a good story, and from what I can tell, Jelly is the story."

"She's *really* the story now that she's gone missing," LuAnn added.

"Gone missing?" A male voice sounded from behind them. Tess turned to discover a handsome man with salt-and-pepper hair wearing a Press badge. He extended his hand and said, "Winston James. I'm a freelance writer for the *Canine Companion.*"

Tess cringed as she realized he had overheard their conversation. She tentatively stuck out her hand. "Nice to meet you."

"Nice to meet you too." As he shook her hand, his brow furrowed. "Did I hear you say that Jelly has gone missing? Are you talking about the cocker spaniel, Angelica?"

Now what? Tess didn't mean to alert the press. She pulled back her hand and decided to change the subject. "Isn't Angelica a beauty? I've had an opportunity to see her up close because she's staying at our inn."

"Oh, you're the owners of Wayfarers?" Now the man really looked intrigued. "Would you mind if I stopped by later today to interview you about the families staying with you? I understand you've got several of the big names at your place."

Ugh. Why did she have to mention that? "Well, we really can't give out any personal information about our guests, you understand," Tess explained. "To be honest, I still haven't quite forgiven LuAnn here for opening up the inn to dogs during the show, anyway."

Why, oh why did she have to open her mouth to say all of that?

"You don't usually have dogs at the inn?" He jotted down a few notes.

"Just Huck, our own dog. But certainly not show dogs like Jelly and Gigi."

"Oh, Gigi's at your place too?" He grinned and jotted down more notes. "The little dachshund who just won her division? You're fortunate to have two beauties in your inn. Quite an honor. You know, there's been an interesting rivalry between those two dogs, even though they're different breeds. Have you picked up on any of that?"

"Oh, I…well…"

LuAnn gave Tess a warning look, but it was too late.

"You know. Just the usual banter. Anyway, we have a full house."

"Who else?"

Of course, Richard Townsen chose that very moment to walk up with Schmaltzy. "Well, hello again, ladies. Who's taking care of the inn if you're both here?"

"Janice," Tess explained.

"Schmaltzy has a grooming appointment with Russ Schumer. We've waited months for this day." He leaned in close. "And you don't even want to know how much I'm paying for this. But my little guy goes into the ring in an hour, and I want him to look perfect."

"Could we go back to talking about the dog that's gone missing?" Winston asked. "Are you helping in the search?"

There was no avoiding the subject now, was there? Tess decided to answer his questions the best she could. "Yes. She slipped out of her crate a few minutes ago. Everyone in the arena is searching."

"Well, I'll be." Winston flipped his notepad closed and jammed his pen into his shirt pocket. "So, it's true. Angelica is missing in action. Coincidence, or are there darker forces at work? Looks like I've got a story to flesh out. The *Canine Companion* will be all over this!"

"Let's not jump the gun." LuAnn shook her head, and for a moment Tess thought she might cluck her tongue at the man. "I wouldn't make too much out of this. When I was a kid I had a Pekingese who ran away at least once a week. He always came back home again."

"Only Jelly is in an unfamiliar place," the reporter countered. "She doesn't know her way around this arena. And her family isn't from Marietta, so if she gets out of the arena she won't know where to go."

"Good point." Richard snapped his fingers, and his eyes lit up. "Hey, maybe she'll find her way back to the inn. I've seen movies where things like that happen."

Tess couldn't imagine that to be possible but decided to give Janice a call, just in case anyone turned up with the dog. She called Janice's number, and her friend answered right away.

"Janice, have you seen Jelly?"

"Jelly...the dog? Or jelly in a jar?"

"Jelly the dog. She's gone missing from the arena."

"No way! I haven't seen any sign of her here, but I'll look outside. Hang on a second." Tess could hear as Janice walked out the front door of the inn. "Here, Jelly! Here, Jelly Bean!" After several attempts, Janice returned to the line. "The only thing I saw was a squirrel. Are you sure she's not still at the arena?"

"Well, she somehow weaseled her way out of her crate, at least that's what we think. She could be in here someplace, hiding. In fact, that would be my guess."

"Man, I hope so. I'd hate to think she slipped out the arena door and into all that traffic."

"Me too. They've got the place under lockdown at the moment, so the doors are being watched. Just say a prayer that they find her, Janice. I feel so bad for the Lawsons."

"Of course. Maybe she's just hiding from them. She seems like a very playful pup."

"True. And she's just a few years old. Still young enough to behave mischievously."

Tess ended the call and turned back toward Winston, who looked as if he wanted to bolt.

"Well, I'd better get back to my...wife. Er, ex-wife. Marigold. Our dog, Horace, is about to compete." He pointed to a crate with a blanket over it. "I'm sure she's pretty wound up. Russ Schumer just groomed Horace, and that always makes her anxious."

"Horace is a girl?" LuAnn asked.

"Horace is a boy. My ex-wife is a girl." He chuckled. "I just meant that she—my ex—is probably getting anxious. But I didn't mean to imply that she was the one who was being groomed."

They all had a good laugh at that one.

"My wife got custody of Horace in the divorce," Winston explained. "She decided to turn him into a show dog. Marigold's wound up tighter than a spring, waiting for the event, so I'd better get over there to calm her down."

Richard then adjusted Schmaltzy's leash. "I've got to get to the grooming area. Say a little prayer for my boy, if you will. He gets so nervous."

"In the ring?" LuAnn asked.

"No, when he's with the groomer." Richard sneezed a couple of times and then took off through the crowd in the direction of the grooming stations.

Winston clucked his tongue. "I hope Russ Schumer doesn't have a grudge against them. He's got a history."

"History?" LuAnn and Tess asked in unison.

"When he gets angry at a family, he takes it out on the dog. That's all. Like what happened with the Lawsons a couple of years ago. You know about that?"

Tess shook her head.

"There was a dispute over the type of cut he gave Angelica a couple of days before her first competition. It blew up. Big. Anyway, let's just say there's been bad blood between Russ and some of his clients and leave it at that."

"A haircut is that big of a deal?" Tess could hardly believe it. "So why is he still in business?"

"Good question. I don't worry about it, because Russ isn't mad at me." He glanced at his watch. "I better get over there and talk to Marigold before the big event. Nice meeting you, ladies."

Winston took off through the mob, and Tess followed him with her gaze. She watched as he hunched down in front of the crate with a blanket on top. There were several ladies seated near his crate, but she couldn't guess which one might be his ex-wife.

"LuAnn, look." She pointed at the crate next to Winston. "His dog's crate is covered up."

"Poor dog is probably panicked because of all the people. If I were a dog you'd have to hang a blanket over my crate too."

Tess took several steps toward Winston and his dog crate. As she drew near, he glanced her way then snatched the crate and took off through the crowd. Very odd. Then again, his dog was competing soon. He said that, right?

Tess found herself within earshot of the groomer, who lifted Schmaltzy to his table. She watched, completely mesmerized, as he began to clip the anxious little dog.

LuAnn pressed her phone back into her purse. "I guess we should get going, Tess. My to-do list is a mile long. I've got a call in to the florist, and she should be calling me back later this afternoon. I've also got to place an order for more paper products. We've almost run out of toilet paper."

Tess couldn't help but laugh at the image that presented. "*That* would be a tragedy."

"Right?"

As they turned to leave, Reena walked toward them with Beauvine in her arms. "My goodness, I've never seen so many dogs together in one place." She shifted Beauvine's position in her arms. "Well, unless you count the Paws on Wheels bus, which is parked just outside. I just came from checking out the transport dogs. That bus is full to the brim." This seemed to get her more excited than ever, and she lit into a lengthy description of all she'd seen—and smelled—inside the bus. "We're done for now," she continued. "But tomorrow's the big day. All the new dog owners will arrive to pick up their pups bright and early tomorrow morning! In the meantime, I've volunteered to serve as hostess in the Paws on Wheels booth, here in the arena. I have to report for duty in an hour and a half."

"That gives you plenty of time to watch Schmaltzy's round first." Richard took a few steps in her direction and gave her an imploring look. "If you would be so kind. We're all alone.

Schmaltzy has no one to root him on, and I'm sure he would be tickled to have the support. I know I would be."

"Well, Beauvine and I would be happy to lend our support." Reena beamed and rested her palm on her chest. "Just tell us where to sit, and we'll be your biggest cheerleaders."

"Just stick with me while he's being groomed. When the time comes, I'll be happy to show you to the best seat in the house." Richard waved his goodbye to Tess and LuAnn, then turned back to the groomer's station with Reena trailing along behind.

"Interesting dynamic between those two," Tess observed.

"Very. I'm glad they've found each other. I suspect they'll become great friends over the next few days."

Before they could expound on the subject, Andy Lawson returned. Tess could tell from the somber expression on his face that he hadn't located Jelly.

"Any luck?" LuAnn asked.

"No." He shook his head. "It's the strangest thing. You'd think someone would have seen her running and playing if she just slipped out of her crate, right?"

"Exactly." LuAnn glanced around, as if expecting the dog to magically appear. "I've been thinking the same thing."

"But literally no one has seen her on the run, which makes me very suspicious."

Tandi and the children approached. Tears streamed down Callie's face as she shared that they still hadn't located Angelica.

"It's okay, honey. We're going to find her." Tandi turned to face Tess and LuAnn. "We were right there, just a few feet away. She couldn't have gone far."

"Maybe you should ask that man." Tess pointed to the groomer with the confident swagger. "He's been here awhile, right? Surely he would have noticed something odd going on nearby."

"You mean Russ Schumer?" Tandi's expression tightened. "I'd rather not." She took hold of her children's hands and muttered a few words under her breath, then headed off to search for Angelica again.

"You have to excuse Tandi," Andy explained. "We had a bit of a mixup with Russ Schumer several years ago. Angelica was about to compete for the first time. Russ claimed my wife asked for a summer cut for Jelly, not a competition cut."

"I heard something about that," Tess said. "It didn't end well?"

"Not really." Andy shook his head. "Anyway, the incident happened in his salon a few days prior to the competition. And, to be fair, Jelly was brand new on the circuit, and Russ had never heard of her before that day, so he didn't realize he was dealing with a show dog."

"Just a mistake, then?" Tess asked, more curious than ever.

"Yes. He claims he didn't get the memo that she was about to compete, so I can see how the mistake might have been made. But Jelly missed out on her first-ever competition and all because of the wrong cut."

"That's awful."

"Lesson learned. We have our own groomer now and only use him when we're at home. Tandi does any necessary touch-ups on competition day. She's gotten really good at it. And, I should add that Russ didn't charge us for the summer cut he gave Jelly.

He felt bad about what happened. He's got an amazing reputation and was so worried we'd make a big deal out of it."

"You didn't?"

"We didn't even though Tandi doesn't like him much." He shrugged. "But someone else did. That writer from the *Canine Companion* wanted to interview us about Jelly, and I agreed. I mentioned the grooming issue—it was the reason she couldn't compete that year, after all—but I asked him not to focus on that in his article. He agreed, but then wrote the story with that slant anyway, even embellishing the facts to make Russ look irresponsible. He made it sound like we were angry and vengeful, which was completely untrue. I was mortified, and so was Tandi. This man could've ruined Russ's reputation. We never wanted that."

"That's awful." Tess shook her head and tried to absorb the information she'd just been given.

"I know. And, to be honest, Jelly was a little young to be competing anyway. So maybe it was a blessing in disguise that she didn't make it into the ring that first year. I even told Winston that when he interviewed me. We've never regretted missing that first year. At least, I know I haven't."

"But he conveniently left that part out of his article?" Tess asked.

Andy nodded. "Sometimes I wonder if we ever should have gotten started down this road at all. Competing is a lot of fun, and it's something the kids are learning to enjoy. But there are some stresses involved, for sure, including jealous competitors who have tried to make our life miserable. And the cost is…"

"Expensive?"

"You have no idea. You've got your entry fees, of course. And travel. And lodging. In our case, lodging for a family of four plus the dog. But then you've also got the other big costs associated with competing—personal trainers, private grooming, vet visits, and so on. It's nuts, really. If you take the time to break it down you see that it's all too much for the average family."

"My goodness." LuAnn looked flabbergasted by all of this. "I'm surprised so many families can keep it up."

"Yes, and many are disappointed in the eleventh hour."

"How so?" she asked.

"Things go wrong at the last minute all the time. You wouldn't believe how many dogs make it right up to the big day and then come down with a stomach bug or something like that. Thousands of dollars spent prepping, only to have to bow out due to illness."

"Does that happen a lot?"

"Well, we've been lucky that Jelly has a cast-iron stomach. Not all dogs do. But you can bet we don't give her anything but the usual food and treats before a big show. We don't want any surprises." He lifted his hands, as if in defeat. "Let's just say I've worked a lot of hours to cover the costs of all this. But it's something we do together as a family, and that's why I keep it up. We're the Lawson team, working together toward one goal, to make Jelly the very best she can be. Win or lose, she's our girl, and we love her."

"I can tell." LuAnn gave him a look of admiration.

"Yes," Tess agreed. "It's so sweet to watch the kids with her."

Just then a voice came over the PA instructing attendees to be on the lookout for a black-and-white cocker spaniel.

Andy startled to attention. "I'm so glad they did that. Now everyone will know she's missing." He sighed. "Guess I'd better get back to the search."

Tess caught a glimpse of Geneva walking Gigi on a leash while trying to balance a covered crate in the other hand.

Andy caught sight of her too and took a few rushed steps in her direction. "Geneva, wait up! I need to ask you a question."

Geneva turned, her face bright red as she nearly lost her grip on the crate. "I'm sorry, but I don't have time right now. There's someplace I have to be. Sorry."

His shoulders sagged as he froze in place.

Geneva turned and took off through the crowd. In fact, she turned so quickly that she jammed the heavy crate into a young woman next to her. The poor woman stepped out of Geneva's way and put her hands up in the air, as if admitting defeat.

"Don't let me get in your way," she yelled as Geneva kept walking.

Geneva hollered a quick apology then disappeared out the front door of the arena.

LuAnn glanced Tess's way, her brow furrowed. "Does something about that feel strange to you?"

"Almost as strange as our interaction with that reporter. I say we get a closer look." Tess rushed to the door of the arena, hot on the heels of one very suspicious competitor.

# CHAPTER FIVE

Tess did her best to keep up with Geneva but lost sight of her as they stepped outside of the arena into the parking lot. She paused and squinted against the glare of the afternoon sun.

"Well, great. Now what?"

"Oh, there she is!" LuAnn pointed.

There, in the east parking lot, Geneva approached her little car. Tess observed as Geneva set the crate on the ground then placed Gigi in some sort of car seat contraption in the front seat on the passenger side. She then picked up the crate and hefted it into the back seat and slammed the door. Then she walked around to the driver's side of the car, where Tess couldn't see her as well.

LuAnn snapped her fingers. "That's it! I've got it!"

"Got what?"

"I've been racking my brain to come up with who Geneva reminds me of, and I think I've finally got it. She looks like a young Nicole Kidman. That long red hair. Thin physique. Pale skin. She's even got some of the same facial expressions."

"I guess you're right, now that I think of it." Tess's words were directed at LuAnn, but her gaze never left Geneva. "Did that crate she just loaded into her back seat look heavy to you? It seemed like she was struggling to lift it."

"Maybe she's got Gigi's things inside."

"Maybe. It's a little weird that she didn't put Gigi in the crate once they got to the car, though. Don't dogs usually ride in crates in cars?"

"Not necessarily." LuAnn laughed. "She has a dog carrier in the front there for Gigi. Listen, I've got some dog-loving friends who allow their dogs to actually sit in their laps while they drive."

"Dangerous." Tess stopped to think. "But something about the way she was handling that crate seemed strange to me, like it was difficult to haul. What if there was another dog inside of it? A little black-and-white cocker spaniel, perhaps?"

"What?" LuAnn looked aghast at this suggestion. "Do you really have reason to believe she would steal Angelica?"

"You heard all of those things she said about Jelly always winning the competition. My imagination might have just kicked into overdrive, but I can see how she would want Jelly out of the competition so Gigi might stand a better chance. Or have I just been watching too many mystery shows on TV?"

"One can never watch too many mystery shows on TV. Let's just clear that up right away."

Tess couldn't help but chuckle at LuAnn's comment. "In spite of the many times we've teased Janice for that very thing?"

"Yes." A smile tipped up the edges of LuAnn's lips as they walked to her car. "But I do love giving her a hard time about it, so let's keep it up."

"Agreed."

"But are you really suggesting that Geneva somehow snuck Jelly into her own dog's crate and waltzed out of the arena with her? Where would she take her? She's a dog lover. I can't picture Geneva harming any dog, even a competitor."

"I don't know, and I'm not saying that she would hurt her. I'm just suggesting she might be getting her out of the competition so Gigi stands a better chance of winning. Something about the way she was acting in there felt strange. She was in a huge hurry to leave. And look at her now. She's rushing to get out of here." Tess pointed as Geneva's car shot backward, nearly hitting another vehicle.

"So what do you want us to do, follow her?"

Something in Tess's gut nudged her forward with the words, "Yes, but we need to hurry, or she's going to get away from us."

"Tess, I can't believe you actually expect me to chase that woman down. What are we going to do if she heads straight back to the inn with Gigi for an afternoon nap? We're going to feel really silly if we follow her and nothing comes of it. And I sure hope she doesn't notice us. That would be awful."

"I hope she *does* go back to the inn, and I also hope that the crate in her back seat is empty. But we won't know any of that unless we stick close to her, right? Just be careful. Don't follow too close."

LuAnn got into the driver's seat, and Tess took her place in the passenger seat beside her. She kept a watchful eye on Geneva's small sedan as the car headed east on Putnam out of the arena area.

LuAnn turned on the car and fiddled with the A/C controls, then backed the car out of the parking space. She eased her SUV through the crowded lot to the exit.

"She turned right on Putnam," Tess said. "But I don't think she's made it very far."

They caught up with her at the first light at the corner of 7th Street.

Tess lowered her voice and ducked down in her seat. "Just don't let her know you're trailing her, LuAnn. And who knows, maybe she'll lead us to more clues."

"I didn't realize we were searching for clues. I thought we were looking for a dog. And why are we whispering?"

"I don't know." Tess shrugged. "I'm afraid she's going to recognize us."

"By the sound of our voices in a separate vehicle?"

"You know what I mean, LuAnn. I have a funny feeling, and when I get these feelings, well…"

"It's time to sit up and pay attention. Got it. And speaking of sitting up, you can sit up now, Tess. The light has changed, and she's moved on. She took a right on 7th."

They followed behind the small gray car for several blocks, past the farmer's market and the gas station. At that point, Geneva turned east on Greene. "I guess we can safely say she's not headed back to the inn." Tess squinted to get a better look as a car eased into the spot between their two vehicles. "I sure hope we don't lose her."

"Don't worry, Tess. I've got this."

A few minutes later, the vehicle turned into a parking lot and they found themselves behind Geneva once again.

"LuAnn, look! She's pulling into that new ice cream shop. I just saw an ad for it in the paper."

"Ice cream sounds good, doesn't it?"

"Very." Tess could almost taste it now, in fact.

LuAnn pulled into the parking lot of a nearby discount tire center, and they watched as Geneva went through the drive-through at the ice cream shop.

"Is she giving that dog ice cream?" Tess rolled down her window in hopes of getting a better look. "Seriously? After all that fussing she did at Winnie over a few scone crumbs?"

"I think this is a case of 'Do as I say, not as I do,'" LuAnn said. "But I wouldn't worry too much. I've seen videos of dogs eating ice cream before. They love it."

Tess squinted and tried to narrow her field of vision to the inside of Geneva's car but couldn't see very well. "Looks like they're getting matching cones. That's one dedicated dog owner. She spoils that dog something awful."

"Man, you can say that again. That dog lives a better life than most of us. But I'll buy you some ice cream if you really want it." LuAnn chuckled.

It did sound good, but there was no time for that now. "Look!" Tess pointed as Geneva's car pulled out of the parking lot. "She's back on the road again."

"Got it, Miss Marple. I'm on the case." LuAnn put her car in gear and took off down the road after her.

"You're losing her, LuAnn!" Tess leaned forward in the seat as the distance between the two cars grew wider. "Drive faster!"

"She's going to figure out I'm tailing her if I get too close. Don't worry, Tess. I can see her just fine from here."

LuAnn eased her way past a car that pulled out in front of them and managed to get behind Geneva's gray sedan once more. Before long, Geneva turned off of the main highway onto a smaller road.

LuAnn followed but kept her distance.

"Why would she be coming all the way out here?" Tess asked. "We're miles from anywhere."

"I have no idea, but she seems to know where she's going."

"We're a long way from the inn. I think I'd better call Janice to give her a heads-up. She's going to be wondering what's taking us so long." Tess punched in Janice's number and then put her on speakerphone.

"Wait. You're where?" Janice asked after Tess's rushed explanation tumbled out.

"Several miles east of town, headed into the country."

"Because…"

"Because we saw Geneva put a dog crate in her car when she left the arena."

"And that raises red flags because…?"

"She has Gigi in the front seat in some sort of carrier, but there appeared to be a crate in the back."

"It could be empty."

"Right, but—Oh!" Tess's voice rose in pitch as Geneva pulled her car into a long driveway leading to a dark green two-story house with broken shutters.

"Now what?" LuAnn tapped the brakes to slow her car. "I can't just pull into someone's driveway."

"Just go down the street a bit and pull over," Tess suggested.

LuAnn did just that. She eased the car onto the shoulder of the road and put it in Park. "Now what, Sherlock?" she asked. "And think twice before you tell me to get out of the car. I might be brave, but I'm not that brave."

"Hello! I'm still here!" Janice's voice sounded from the other end of the phone. "I don't think it's safe to get out of the car if you two are alone. Just turn around and come back to the inn. It's not worth it, Tess."

"Roger Wilco. Headed home." LuAnn reached for the gearshift.

Tess ended the call and sighed. "I guess she's right. I feel foolish, dragging us all the way out here to the woods."

"Let's just forget about it. It's none of our business, anyway."

LuAnn eased the car forward until she found a small driveway. Then she pulled in and turned the car around. As they passed back by the house where Geneva had pulled in, Tess put her hand up. "LuAnn, slow down." Off in the distance the distinct sound of barking dogs filled the air. She rolled down her window, and the barking intensified. "Do you hear that?"

"Yes, Gigi's pretty yappy, but that sounds like a lot of dogs, not just one or two."

Their conversation ended, but the barking did not. The echo of multiple dogs barking filled the air. Gigi definitely wasn't the only dog in attendance at this meeting. If the yaps were any indication, she was one of many.

"What sort of place is this?" LuAnn inched the car forward until they had a better view of the house.

Tess caught a glimpse of Geneva standing in the driveway. She appeared to be arguing with an older woman who held a small tan dog in her arms. The barking continued but so did the yelling. The woman was having it out with Geneva, or maybe it was the other way around.

"Ugh! Can you roll the window back up, please?" LuAnn waved her hand in front of her face. "Something smells awful."

The odor was pretty nasty, Tess had to admit. She rolled up her window and leaned back against the seat. "I think we'd better get out of here. I have a bad feeling."

"Me too," LuAnn agreed as she eased the car forward.

Just as they reached the edge of the property, Tess caught a glimpse of something through the trees. "LuAnn, look!" She pointed to a row of chain-link fences in the side yard. She couldn't help but gasp aloud as dogs came into view—dozens and dozens of dogs. "Stop the car."

"What?"

"Stop the car!" Tess had the door handle pulled before LuAnn even came to a complete stop.

"Are you crazy? You can't get out here. You might get shot. You watch True Crime shows, Tess. You know what could happen. Don't you dare—"

Tess didn't hear the rest of what LuAnn had to say. She had already crossed the road and was trying to maneuver the ditch. She slogged her way through some mud then squeezed past the bushes to the first row of chain-link fences. Her heart jumped to her throat when she locked her eyes on the layout of the dog pens. How could so many dogs exist, crammed together like this?

They were divided by breed, at least they appeared to be. And when the poor emaciated pooches saw her, they went crazy with excitement. Many jumped on the fences, begging to be let out.

"Shh." She put her finger to her lips. "Quiet!"

She could barely look at them without wanting to cry. The ones with longer fur were so matted she couldn't even make out the breed. A few had obvious ailments or deformities. She felt sick inside as she looked at them. Many of their little mouths were bleeding. She could see why as soon as she realized they were chewing on the chain-link fence in an attempt to free themselves.

Her heart twisted as she stared in disbelief at the scene in front of her. "How could anyone do this to you?"

The dogs answered with pitiful moans that broke her heart.

When she glanced down once again, Tess realized that all of the water bowls were completely empty. She couldn't help herself. Something had to be done. She whispered the words, "I'll be right back," then rushed back to the car and flung open the door.

"Give me your water bottle."

"What?" LuAnn stared at her, wide-eyed. "Why?"

"I need it, LuAnn, and mine too."

"Why? What's happened? Is it bad?"

"Bad?" Tess shook her head and forced the tears down. "It's not just bad, LuAnn. It's the worst thing I've seen in years. I had no idea a place like this existed so close to where we live.

It's everything awful you've ever been told about puppy mills and much, much more. Truly horrible. Like, 'Call the police right now' horrible." Tears sprang to her eyes. "How anyone could neglect animals like this is beyond me."

"I've got to see this for myself."

The idea of getting caught brought a wave of fear over Tess. She shook her head. "No. Please don't. What if Geneva passes by us? She'll recognize our car. I say we just get out of here, once and for all."

"It's not likely she'll know our car. We're practically strangers. But just in case, I'll pull off the road." LuAnn found a shaded area in the gravel next to the road. "I'm going to take my phone so I can get some pictures. If it's as bad as you say, we'll need proof of what we've seen for the police. And I'll need the address of this house too."

"You can pull up the address on your maps app on your phone. But quick, let's get behind the bushes so no one will see us."

"Okay, but give me a minute. I always keep extra water in the back." LuAnn popped the back of the SUV and pulled out several bottles, which she handed to Tess. Then she grabbed a few more.

As they crossed the road toward the ditch, Tess's stomach felt as if it plummeted to her toes. In fact, she was hit with the realization that they were trespassing. What if the owner of the puppy mill approached them? Worse still, what if she had a gun? The woman arguing with Geneva didn't look like someone Tess would ever want to mess with.

Still, these little dogs needed help, and they needed it now. She would muster up the courage and give them water, at the very least.

"Ugh! I stepped in mud." LuAnn groaned as they tromped across the ditch. She lifted her leg to reveal her shoes caked in wet mud.

"Sorry, I should have warned you about that. Follow me, LuAnn." Tess led the way through the bushes, and before long they were in front of the fenced area once more.

They eased their way through the brush into the area where the chain-link fences began. LuAnn stopped cold when she saw the dogs.

"Oh, Tess." She scrambled to open a water bottle and then opened the gate and stepped inside the fenced area, where they began the process of pouring water into the filthy bowls. Then she began to take pictures of the dogs, one section after another. On and on they went, until they heard someone whistle and call out a dog's name.

"What's going on over here?" The woman's words were laced with anger. "You mutts need to keep it down!"

Tess put her finger to her lips and took a couple of steps backward. She mouthed the words, "Let's go!" and then took off toward the road, empty water bottles in hand. A couple of them fell to the ground, but Tess kept running. Only when she heard the owner's angry voice cry out again did the panic hit her. Her legs had never moved so fast.

LuAnn followed behind her, away from the animals and toward the bushes near the road. Just as they nudged their way through the brush, Geneva's car zoomed by. Tess hid herself to keep from being noticed. When she was sure they were safe, she stepped out onto the road. Her breath came in shallow spurts as she crossed the road.

"I—I—never—ran—that fast—before!"

"Me neither." LuAnn reached into her pocket for the car keys and popped the back of the vehicle. They tossed their empty bottles inside, and LuAnn got behind the wheel. She leaned her head back and erupted in tears. "What. In. The. World?" She hit her head against the back of the seat as if trying to knock what she'd seen away for good.

"It's cruel. And abusive. We've got to do something, LuAnn, but what? Who do we call?"

"The police, that's who. We have no choice. We have to involve them. Whoever did this has to go to jail. And those animals need to be re-homed as soon as possible."

"I agree. Can I just glance at the pictures you took before we call? I just need to make sure it was really as bad as I think it was so I know how to describe it."

LuAnn pressed her phone into Tess's hand and muttered, "It was worse, Tess. A lot worse."

"I'm so glad you thought to take the pictures. I was so frazzled, it didn't even occur to me."

"I had to do it. I'm not sure anyone would have believed us otherwise. It's beyond comprehension."

Tess opened the photo app and scrolled through the pictures, her stomach churning as she saw the images pop up on the screen. "This poor little dog with the infected eye!" She held up the phone for LuAnn to see. "I just feel so sorry for him. And the one with the broken leg? How could anyone leave them like that, day after day?"

"I would guess they've had no veterinary care at all."

"I probably won't be able to sleep tonight," Tess said as she turned her attention away from the photos. "If I do, I'll have nightmares."

"Me too." LuAnn grew silent for a moment, then finally asked the question both of them had been thinking: "What in the world was Geneva doing at a place like that?"

"I have no idea," Tess countered. "But I won't rest until I find out."

# CHAPTER SIX

Tess's heartbeat drummed in her ears as they pulled away from the broken-down house in the woods. She couldn't shake the images she'd just seen of dirty, matted dogs behind chain-link fences.

LuAnn was silent for a while but finally spoke. "That's the first puppy mill I've seen—or smelled—up close."

"Me too. Now I see why Jordan has such strong opinions about them. Those poor dogs looked miserable. Why in the world would that woman keep them in such deplorable conditions?"

"No idea, but I know for a fact the county will take the dogs away from them." LuAnn turned right onto a major thoroughfare and pointed the car back in the direction of the inn. "There are organizations that specialize in things like that."

"Paws on Wheels?"

"I'm not sure if they take mill dogs, but we can ask Jordan. He might be able to advise us." She sniffed the air. "What am I smelling?"

"I suspect it's our feet." Tess lifted her foot to examine the bottoms of her shoes. "Ugh. That's not just mud we stepped in, I'm afraid."

"Ugh. I love these shoes too. I've only worn them a few times."

"Sorry about that." One thing still had Tess stumped. "I still can't figure out why Geneva would go to a place like that."

"Are you still thinking she had Angelica in that crate in her back seat? Is there any chance at all she was dropping her off there?"

"No, I don't think so." Tess shook her head. "I'm more inclined to think she's buying another dog. Maybe that's why she went there."

LuAnn groaned aloud. "If she buys it from that horrible place, I hope she'll bathe it before bringing that odor into Wayfarers. Can you imagine?"

"No." Tess lost herself to her thoughts for a moment. "And I hope Reena doesn't find out that Geneva's doing business with a puppy mill. She and Jordan will flip if they hear that a fellow guest at the inn is connected to one of those places."

LuAnn wrinkled her nose. "I saw enough to last me a lifetime. The smell was enough to knock me backward. I didn't capture that on film, thank goodness, though I'm sure my clothes reek. And there had to have been a hundred dogs, easy."

LuAnn tapped on the brakes as they neared a major intersection. "Geneva definitely won't have a chance to buy anything from that breeder. They'll shut that mill down in a hurry."

"True." Tess reached for her own phone. "I just need to figure out who to call. Animal control? The police?" She tried to do a search on her phone, but the signal was too weak. After several futile attempts she finally shoved the phone back into her purse. "I'll take care of it as soon as we get home. Don't let me forget."

"As if I could."

As they drove the rest of the way, Tess and LuAnn tried to make sense out of what they'd seen. They arrived back at the inn a few minutes later. Both of them pulled off their dirty shoes in the mudroom off of the kitchen and then entered the inn in bare feet. Once inside, Tess telephoned the police station, and Officer Randy Lewis answered. She didn't have long to share about the puppy mill but gave what few details she could remember, including the address.

"We've got photos galore," she explained. "They're all digital. Should we send them?"

Randy gave her an email address to send them to, along with several reassurances that he would take this information seriously. "I'll contact Animal Control first thing in the morning," he said. "And I'll tell Chief Mayfield about your call. This case will likely involve county officials."

"Thank you."

"No, thank you. But do me a favor. Next time don't go onto someone else's property. It's just too dangerous. You never know how a homeowner might respond if they find someone on their land."

"I promise."

"I'm just looking out for you," he said. "Better safe than sorry. I've seen these stories end badly."

"I'm sure." At the last minute, Tess decided to share one last bit of information with the officer. "I know you guys are on the hunt for a missing dog named Angelica," she said. "I'm not saying you'll find her at that puppy mill. I just think it would be wise to keep your eyes open, just in case."

"Will do."

She ended the call, then she and LuAnn went in search of Janice. They found her in the office, hard at work on the computer. Tess couldn't help but notice Huck, sleeping in the corner of the room. Good old Huck, ever present. Janice swiveled around in the chair to face them, eyes widening as their story spilled out.

"Remind me again why you went traipsing off in the woods after one of our guests in the first place?"

Tess sighed. "It's my fault. I had a feeling."

"Ah, a feeling. Well, that explains it."

"Hey," Tess countered. "I get those feelings sometimes, and they pan out to be something."

Janice crossed her arms at her chest. "Well, the next time you get one, please contact the police right away so that they can help you. Promise?"

"I promise. And just for the record, Randy Lewis scolded me for the very same thing."

"Good. Because I would hate to see my two best friends shot in the woods." She lit into a lecture about how foolish their actions had been. When she finally calmed down, Janice turned back to her computer. "While you were gone, I did a little sleuthing of my own. I've been researching that groomer, Russ Schumer."

LuAnn rounded the desk to look at the computer screen. "Find anything?"

"Several complaints with the Better Business Bureau."

"About his grooming style?"

"One of them, but most were about his temper."

"Temper?"

"From what I read, he's very temperamental with the dog owners. Demanding. Several people said they got talked into extra services they hadn't asked for. That sort of thing."

Tess snorted. "And yet he's one of the most requested groomers out there."

"Right."

A noise in the lobby alerted the ladies to the fact that someone had just entered, which shut the conversation down.

They walked out to discover that the Lawson family had just entered the front door. Little Callie looked like she'd been crying. For that matter, so did her mother. Tandi's eyes were swollen and bloodshot. The usually feisty Wyatt plopped down on the sofa and buried his head in a pillow. The poor kid looked exhausted. Huck sauntered in the direction of the children and nuzzled his head against Callie's leg. She petted him then knelt down to hug him.

Tess took several steps toward the family as she saw Andy come through the door with a dog crate in hand. "Did you find her?"

He shook his head. "No. We contacted the police and everyone in the arena is still on high alert. She has a microchip, so we can only hope and pray that someone finds her and turns her in."

"I would never have dreamed something like this could happen at a competition." Tandi took a seat next to her son on the sofa. Her nose wrinkled, and she sniffed the air. "What is that smell?" Her gaze shifted down to Tess's and LuAnn's bare feet. Janice and LuAnn excused themselves and headed toward the kitchen.

Before Tess could explain, Callie cried out, "Mama! I want my Jelly Bean back!"

"Of course you do, baby." Tandi knelt and comforted her daughter. "We all do. Angelica is part of the family." She turned her gaze to Tess and continued. "Jelly's like one of my kids. The competing, that's fun, of course, but Jelly will always be a winner, even if she didn't compete. She's our little girl."

At this point, Callie erupted in tears. She rushed to the sofa and threw herself down.

Tandi drew near and slipped her arm around her daughter's shoulders. "I'm just kicking myself because I was the last one to mess with the crate. I usually slide both locks closed, but this time I think I only locked the top one. It's possible it just came loose, and she got out."

"I checked and double-checked those latches." Andy's gaze traveled down to the crate in his hand. "They're in perfect order."

Tandi sighed. "Then I don't know what could have happened, unless..." Her words trailed off, and tears brimmed her lashes.

"I'll be praying someone turns her in." These were the only words of comfort Tess could think to speak.

Andy gave her a look of gratitude then turned to face his children. "I think it's time for you kiddos to take a bath and get ready for bed. We've had a long day."

The children rose from the sofa and took a few steps toward him. He stepped in the direction of the elevator.

Andy shifted the crate to his other hand. Apparently it was heavy, even when empty. Tess's thoughts soared back to Geneva, who had hefted a crate into the back seat of her car. Maybe there was no dog in it, after all.

"I want you to know how grateful we are for your prayers that we'll find Jelly."

"Of course," Tess said. "I'm always happy to pray."

"That's where answers are found."

He joined his family in the elevator, and the doors closed. Seconds later, the front door of the inn opened, and Geneva stepped inside with Gigi, who was strangely without attire. The usually well-put-together Geneva looked frazzled.

The hair on the back of Tess's neck prickled. She forced a smile as she greeted her. "Glad to have you back. How was your day?"

"Oh, my day?" Geneva's face flushed, and her gaze shifted to the floor then back up again. "Fine. Fine."

"I saw you go by at the arena when I was talking to Andy Lawson. You seemed to be in a hurry."

"Yes, I was. Well, I had to get to..." Her words drifted off. "I had something to take care of. It was very important. Very." Her nose wrinkled. "I smell something...odd."

"Oh?" Tess changed the subject. "I heard Gigi did well in her round this morning."

At once, all the concern vanished from Geneva's face. Her eyes lit with merriment as she reached down to scoop her baby into her arms. "Yes, she's amazing. And we're so excited about the Best in Show round on Saturday. Can't wait, in fact. Will you be there?"

"I hope to be there."

Her gaze went to the floor again, and for a moment, Tess thought the woman looked as if she might cry. "Well, I'd better be going up to my room now. I'm awfully tired."

"I'll bet." Tess stopped short of saying more. "Well, have a good night, you and Gigi both."

"Thanks."

Geneva headed upstairs, and Tess turned to walk into the kitchen, where she found LuAnn and Janice seated at the kitchen table, talking about wedding plans. They grew quiet the moment she entered.

"Hey, don't stop on my account," Tess said. "I don't mind."

"No, I'd rather hear more about your adventures today. LuAnn was showing me the pictures." Janice waved her hand in front of her face. "And I caught a big whiff of both of you coming in. It's going to take a very long shower to get rid of that aroma."

"No kidding. I need to get upstairs and take one, for sure."

"Definitely," Janice said. "But, before you do, tell me how this puppy mill is linked to the dog that's missing. Or is it?"

"I honestly don't know. At first we thought Geneva might have taken her there, but now that doesn't make sense." Tess poured a cup of decaf and took a seat at the table with her friends.

"Maybe she didn't take her there," LuAnn said. "But we need to at least consider the possibility that someone might have taken off with her—either to get her out of the competition before the big round on Saturday, or to get revenge on the family."

"Revenge…for what?" Janice asked.

"We can't figure that part out." LuAnn rose and walked to the sink. She rinsed out her coffee cup and set it down. "I guess a case could be made that someone—take Geneva, for example—wanted Jelly out of the competition because she's won Best in Show a couple of years in a row."

"Oh!" Tess snapped her fingers. "That freelance writer told me that the dog groomer had some sort of beef against the Lawsons a few years back. Then Andy told me that the guy wrote an article blaming Russ Schumer for ruining Jelly's chances at her first competition. I think the article did some damage to his reputation."

"Were the Lawsons responsible for the article?" Janice asked.

"I don't think so." Tess struggled to remember what she'd heard. "In fact, Andy acted like he didn't mind at all that Jelly missed out on her first competition. He said she wasn't ready."

"Hmm." Janice took a sip of her coffee. "Doesn't sound like a vendetta, then."

"No, surely not."

The bell alerted them to the fact that someone else had entered the front door of the inn. The ladies sprang into action. LuAnn led the way into the foyer, where they discovered

Richard Townsen with Reena at his side. Reena was all smiles as she set Beauvine down.

"What a day we've had." The cutest little giggle escaped as she glanced Richard's way. "I met so many wonderful people. There are so many dog lovers out there. Oh, we had a blast!"

"Well, good evening, you two." Tess laughed. "Or should I say, you four."

LuAnn pointed at the dogs. "How did it go today, Richard? Did Schmaltzy have a good day at the competition?"

"Thanks for asking. He came in third in his breed, but performed well." Richard leaned down and scooped the little pup into his arms. Schmaltzy licked him on the nose. "I don't care anything about winning or losing. We're just in this to have fun and to meet people."

To his left, Reena cleared her throat.

A smile turned up the edges of Richard's lips. "Yes, and speaking of that, Schmaltzy has made a new friend too. Check out these two." He set his dog down, and the little schnauzer went straight to Beauvine and started wagging his tail. "They're best buds, even though they've just met." Richard reached for the box of tissues and dabbed at his nose then coughed a couple of times.

"Sometimes it's like that." Reena gave Richard a warm smile. "You meet someone for the first time, and it's like you've known them forever."

"Don't you love it when that happens?" He gazed her way, and for a moment everything froze. It reminded Tess of a scene from an old black-and-white movie she'd watched recently.

Then, just as quickly, Richard and Reena broke the silence with more giggles. *Okay, then.*

Janice glanced at her watch. "Is the competition just now getting over?"

"Oh, heavens, no," Reena said. "They wrapped up hours ago."

"We got a little distracted," Richard said. "She talked me into going over to meet the nicest fellow—a man who runs a dog rescue organization. Next thing you know I'm on the bus meeting the dogs and their rescuer. We had the best conversation over dinner at a lovely restaurant."

"Did I forget to thank you for dinner?" Reena gazed up at him with puppy dog eyes. "I know Jordan and his wife were tickled pink to have a night out."

"Happy to be of service." He gave Reena an admiring look. "This woman here is something else, I tell you. They're making a film about their journey with the shelter dogs, and she was up there in front of the camera like a pro."

"So it went well?" Tess asked.

Reena nodded enthusiastically. "Terrific! Jordan introduced me to the media team he hired to shoot the film. We spent a couple of hours taking photos and videos of me with the dogs. Tomorrow morning is when they'll be on site to get the best shots of the families taking their new pets home. They're going to use them in the documentary. Oh, I can't wait!"

"We saw the Paws on Wheels van in the arena parking lot when we first arrived," LuAnn said. "It all sounds so exciting."

"Oh, it is. There's so much to look forward to."

She batted her eyes in Richard's direction, and his face lit in a smile.

"It was a little crazy on our end." Tess stifled a yawn. "What with Jelly disappearing and all."

"Jelly? That's the dog they were talking about on the PA, that precious little pup who's staying on the second floor with me?" Reena clasped a hand to her mouth and then pulled it away. "Oh, tell me it's not so. What happened? Tell me, please."

"From what I understand, the Lawson family was in the competitor's lounge, right next to the groomer's area," LuAnn explained. "They were resting and visiting with friends, I believe. Mrs. Lawson turned around to check on the dog, and her crate was empty."

"She busted out? Beauvine does that all the time." Reena began to fuss about her dog's penchant for running away. "There's probably something wrong with the latch on the crate. Either that, or Jelly's stronger than you know."

"Maybe," Janice responded. "But the crate seems to be fine, according to Mr. Lawson."

"That's awful news, just awful." Reena's eyes filled with tears as she leaned down to pick up her feisty little pup. "I don't know what I'd ever do if anything happened to Beauvine. He's like my..."

"Your baby." Richard scooped Schmaltzy into his arms and cuddled him. "I understand. They're really like our kids, aren't they?"

"For sure." She gave Beauvine a kiss on the top of his head.

Tess found the whole thing rather sweet.

LuAnn's cell phone rang. She pulled it out of her pocket, glanced down at it, and excused herself to the kitchen. No doubt Brad was calling for his usual end-of-day chat with her.

"I can't wait for tomorrow morning. The shelter dogs are going to their forever homes." Reena gave Janice and Tess an imploring look. "Will you be there? It's going to be wonderful."

"I wish I could, but I have a busy morning," Janice explained. "I'm up to my eyeballs in work for the inn, and I need to take care of some personal things for my son and future daughter-in-law as well."

"You, Tess?" Reena looked Tess squarely in the eye.

Before she could stop herself, Tess was nodding. "Sure, I'd love to see you in action, Reena. Sounds like fun."

"Bless you! You can ride with us. Richard is driving me over so Jordan doesn't have to come and fetch me. He's got enough on his plate after all. We'll be leaving around eight thirty, so be dressed and ready!"

Tess gave her a thumbs-up.

Richard and Reena boarded the elevator together, still talking about the events of their day.

Tess waited until the elevator door closed to share her thoughts with Janice, who looked just as pleased as she did by the blossoming friendship between their two older guests. "Well now, that's something. Was it my imagination or was Reena flirting?"

"She was." Janice nodded. "It's just so sweet. Two senior citizens, brought together over their love of dogs."

"Yes, I guess that's pretty undeniable."

Tess glanced across the room at Huck, who lay curled up next to the leg of the sofa. As she watched him snore on the rug, unusual feelings tugged at her heartstrings.

"What are you thinking about, Tess?" Janice asked. "You've got the oddest look on your face."

"Just thinking about Huck, about how I look at him more as a staple around here."

"A staple?"

"You know what I mean. He's just part of the everydayness. I get up in the morning, and he greets me with his tail wagging. I take him out for a walk, and he leads me around like he owns the world. I don't really take the time to think of him as this amazing, beloved child. Is it weird that my relationship with dogs isn't like everyone else's?"

"First of all, there are probably more people who feel like you than folks who baby their dogs like our current guests do."

"Like Geneva, you mean?" Even as Tess spoke Geneva's name aloud, memories of what she and LuAnn had witnessed earlier resurrected. A chill ran down her spine as she thought about that puppy mill.

"Yes." Janice nodded again. "Let's just get that straight. I'm all for loving your pets, but she's a little over-the-top for me. I think her issues run a little deeper than the usual pet lover's."

"Meaning?"

"Meaning, maybe she's struggling with a little bit of loneliness. Who knows? She carries her pet-loving to excess."

"Maybe, but you get my point. I guess what I'm saying is that I take Huck for granted. He's just...here. And I don't often take the time to really play with him or love on him. You know? To me, he's like part of the furniture, not a living, breathing thing that demands my attention or excessive affection."

"Is this a confession?" Janice asked.

"Not really. And, don't get me wrong. I love him." Tess glanced down at Huck, who must have picked up on the fact that she was talking about him. His tail *thump-thumped* on the floor. "It's just not the dress-him-up-and-take-him-out-for-a-movie-and-dinner kind of love. It's more the you-sit-over-there-and-I'll-sit-over-here kind."

"Nothing wrong with that."

"I see how these folks are with their dogs, and I just feel like maybe Huck's getting a raw deal, getting stuck with someone like me."

Janice put her hands on her hips. "Are you kidding me? Do you see how much attention that dog gets from the people who come in and out of here? Just this morning I saw Reena slip him one of Beauvine's treats. And don't even get me started on Thorn. He's occasionally been known to stop off at the butcher to pick up special cuts of meat for Huck."

"He does?"

"Yes. And if you're worried he's not getting enough affection, you can stop fretting over that too. Think about the hundreds of times guests have come through here raving over him. He's spoiled rotten by guests and locals alike."

"I guess you're right." Tess stifled a yawn. "Oh my goodness, did I really just tell Reena that I would go with her to the Paws on Wheels event at eight thirty in the morning?"

"Pretty sure that's what I heard you say."

Tess groaned. "How does she do it? She has a way about her, doesn't she? First she gets me to commit to donating, and now I'm showing up at the event. Next thing you know, I'll be the official dog bather."

"Hey, it's a worthy cause," LuAnn chimed in as she reentered the room, phone in hand. "Check out the Paws on Wheels website, and you'll see what amazing work they do for those dogs." She lifted her phone. "But I need to run something by you before you head up to bed. That was Brad on the phone. He's asked me out to breakfast in the morning. We won't take long, probably just an hour or so. Are you okay with that, Janice? Robin will be here to help, so I think the breakfast crowd will be covered. I'll be back in time to help with our lunch guests."

Janice seemed to take the news in stride. "No problem. I'm sure we will manage. Breakfast crowds have been lighter than usual with the dog show going on. So many of our regulars are at the arena."

"Right. Well, thank you."

Tess felt her eyes growing heavy. "I'm exhausted. It's been a long day, ladies, and I need my beauty sleep."

They headed up the stairs together. When they got to the second floor, the sound of crying stopped them in their tracks.

The wails were coming from the Lawsons' room. In that moment, as she thought about all they had lost, Tess's heart twisted. No sooner did she feel her own eyes begin to water than she looked down and noticed Huck was coming up the stairs with them. He was their ever-faithful companion these days, wasn't he?

She reached down and patted him on the head. "You know what, sweet boy? You can sleep in my room tonight—but just this once."

# CHAPTER SEVEN

*April 3, 1862*

With the help of her husband, Prudence managed to get the Union soldier inside their home. They got him settled into a bed, and she tended to his wounded shoulder. The injury was deep—so deep that it took her breath away.

He cried out in pain, and the dog, his ever-faithful companion, rushed to his bedside, as if to warn Prudence to take care with his friend. The poor man cried out as she worked on him.

"How bad is it, Pru?" Jason asked.

"Deep, and badly infected, but I think I can help. Get me that salve from the kitchen cabinet, Jason. I will need boiling water and rags as well. And while thee is there, will thee stir the stew that's on the stove?"

"Of course. I will be right back." He disappeared out of the room, and she covered the man's wound with his shirt. He groaned and reached with his opposite hand to grab his shoulder. She pulled his hand back, and he fought her.

"Thee must not touch it," she warned. "It is badly infected. Let it be so I can tend to it."

The man's eyes fluttered open for the first time, and she saw they were a deep blue, the color of the plates in the kitchen cupboard, a stark contrast to his fair skin.

"What is thy name?" she asked.

"Nate, ma'am. Short for Nathaniel." He shifted his position in the bed and groaned.

"Easy, Nate."

"You don't understand. I can't stay here. I'm under orders to get that dog to Philadelphia."

"Philadelphia?"

"Yes." The man moaned and tried to sit up in the bed but was unable. He settled back against the pillows and fought to keep his eyes open. "You see, Jack here means the world to us. He's been a mascot for our 103rd Division for some time."

"A mascot?"

The man nodded and flinched as his shoulder moved. "He kept morale up, for sure. Such a smart boy. My friend Alex trained him to understand bugle calls and how to search for fallen comrades on the field."

Prudence gave the dog an admiring look.

Nate's lips curled downward. "Alexander lost his life in service to his country. That's why we're trying to get Jack to Philadelphia, to his family's place. It's the least we can do. We think the dog would be a great comfort to his parents."

Ah. It was starting to make sense now. Her heart went out to all of the ones missing poor Alex, including the dog in front of her now. Still, this man was in no shape to transport anyone or anything. Not now. Not like this. "Thee has taken him as far as thee can," she said. "Thee will have to trust thy passengers to get him the rest of the way. I am sure they would be honored."

"Oh no, ma'am. I can't risk it. I've got to deliver him myself." The poor fellow fought to sit up but fell back again as the pain took hold. "I've got to do what's right for Alex's family. Will you watch Jack for me until I'm healed up enough to move on?"

"Watch him for thee? That big dog? I have got a little boy to tend to, my Moses. I fear that dog is bigger than he is and would scare him to death."

"Jack wouldn't hurt a flea, let alone a little boy. He'll be good for your son, I promise. And besides, that old dog needs you, ma'am. I'm afraid he's not doing well. Look at his back leg, and you'll see what I mean."

He called the dog to come toward the bed, and for the first time Prudence could see that the poor thing's back left leg was injured. Had he been hurt in the skirmish too?

Jason came back in the room with the water, salve, and rags. "Here you go, Pru." He glanced down at Nate. "Well now, thee is awake, soldier. Welcome to Marietta."

"Promise me," Nate begged, eyes squinted in pain. "Promise you'll take care of Jack until I'm well enough to take him on."

"Take care of Jack?" Jason looked back and forth between the man and Prudence, clearly confused.

Prudence gave her husband a glance that said, "We will talk about it later," and he didn't say another word. Instead, he helped her tend to Nate's wounds, then offered to go back to the kitchen for a bowl of beef stew for their patient.

Nate dozed off after eating, and Prudence did what she could to help the dog's wounded leg. She cleaned and treated it, then wrapped it in strips of cloth. Afterward, Prudence walked back into the kitchen with the soldier's now-empty bowl.

"Will thee keep an eye on him while I tend to the others?" she asked.

"I am happy to help as best I can, but promise me thee will be careful, Pru."

"I will, I promise."

Jason rose and took the bowl from her hand. He glanced down at the dog, who tagged along on her heels. "What do we do with *him?*"

She looked down at the dog and groaned. "Shoo now, boy. Thee cannot be in here. This kitchen is off-limits."

Jack walked to the edge of the kitchen and curled up in a ball then settled against the wall.

"Ooh, dog!" Moses set his bowl of stew aside and walked over to Jack. Before long, Jack was licking the little boy on the face. Probably just the smell of the stew, but the youngster acted as if they were best friends.

Prudence got to work washing the bowls. The dog looked at her with such intensity, it broke her heart. She could read the hunger in his eyes. He began to whimper, and she couldn't take it anymore.

"Well, just one bite won't hurt you." She tossed a little nibble of the meat his way, and he caught it in midair, which caused Moses to giggle with delight.

This only served to energize the dog. Before long he was at her side, tail wagging.

"Fine, fine." Prudence wiped her palms on her apron and walked over to the far side of the room. The scraps of meat she'd tossed aside—mostly fat and gristle—were quickly gathered together onto a piece of cloth, which she placed on the ground. The dog devoured all of it in a hurry. She then filled an old wooden bowl with water and placed it on the ground for him to drink. Prudence had never seen a dog so thirsty.

Jason turned his attention to Moses and the wounded soldier while Prudence gathered food, coffee, and water for their guests waiting for her at the inn. She made her way to where they were hiding, then led them to safe quarters below the inn where she fed them then gave them blankets for sleeping.

"We thank you, miss," Abram said as he settled back against the blanket with a deep yawn. "And I'm praying for that soldier. He looked to be in mighty poor condition."

"I will do my best to help him, but those prayers will help."

After she wrapped up her work with her guests, Prudence lugged the dirty dishes home. As she made the trek, she struggled with what to do with the dog. He didn't really give her a choice. Wherever she went, he followed.

When she arrived at home, she found Jason dressing Moses for bed.

He pointed to the dog, now curled up asleep on the edge of the rug.

"I know, I know." She wiped her hands on her apron. "He wants to stay."

"He is bigger than the house. Certainly bigger than our boy."

"When thee hears his story, I promise thee will not mind if he stays."

"He is staying outside, though?"

She shook her head. "We cannot run the risk of him running off to find his owner. This dog is heading north as soon as that soldier is well enough."

"That could take days, or weeks."

"I know, Jason. But please. He is such a sweet thing."

Jason stared at the gentle giant, who shook off his slumber and rose to four legs. "Pru, that is the biggest dog I have ever seen in my life."

For certain, she could not argue with him on that point.

# CHAPTER EIGHT

The inn seemed quieter than usual on Wednesday night. Either Gigi was exhausted, or she'd given up on the idea that barking through the night would get her anywhere. Tess slept like a rock, waking only once when she heard the elevator at around four in the morning.

She arose at her usual time and went to work in the kitchen helping Winnie, who still looked half-asleep as she pulled a tray of muffins out of Big Red.

"You okay over there?" Tess asked as she reached for a coffee cup.

"Mm-hmm. Couldn't sleep last night. Someone's dog yapped all night long. Drove me nuts."

"Your neighbors have a dog? I've never heard you mention it before."

"I've never heard it before, and I'm not sure who to blame." She shrugged and continued on with her work. "The new owners use the home as a vacation rental, so people have been coming and going from it. You know the one I'm talking about?"

"I do. It's one of those really cute cottages."

"Most of the time it doesn't bother me, but this time I guess the guests brought a dog. I don't recall that ever happening before." She yawned. "Probably one of the competitors from the dog show. I'll just have to tough it out until the competition is over, but it's wrecking my sleep patterns."

"That's a shame, but I can certainly relate."

"Mm-hmm. I hope I can stay awake this morning to feed this crowd."

"We'll help. But I did want to remind you I'm leaving with Reena and Richard at eight thirty. We have to be at the arena by nine for the big Welcome Home party."

"Welcome Home party?" Winnie looked perplexed.

"The Paws on Wheels dogs are all going to their new homes today, and a film crew will be there to catch the story. I think our local news media will be there as well."

"Ugh. Dogs. Did you have to go and say that word?" Winnie pulled the apple crumble muffins from their tins and placed them on a cooling rack. She muttered under her breath about the dog that had kept her up all night.

"Sorry!" Tess filled a cup with coffee, then settled down at the table.

A couple of minutes later Janice walked into the kitchen and reached for a coffee mug. She took one look at Winnie and shook her head. "You look beat."

"I'm peopled out."

"And dog-tired." Tess laughed. "Hey, that was punny."

For the first time all morning, Winnie actually cracked a smile.

"I understand being exhausted." Janice covered her mouth as a little yawn escaped. "I love the inn, don't get me wrong, but there are times when I'm awfully glad I have my own space, way up on the fourth floor. At least I don't have to go very far to get away from the chaos and confusion."

At that point, the yapping began from upstairs. Tess fought the temptation to roll her eyes. "Maybe we should look into putting better insulation between the floors."

"They'll be gone soon, Tess." Janice gave her a sympathetic look. "Are you okay?"

"What do you mean?"

"I mean, you seem a little tense lately. Are you upset with LuAnn for coming up with this idea to open our doors to dogs during the competition?"

Tess sighed. "Look, I don't want to be difficult. I think I'm just a little stressed because I'm not used to so many dogs underfoot."

"And I'm busy with Stuart and Zelda." Janice paused, and her eyes filled with compassion. "I'm sure that isn't helping."

"I hadn't even thought about that. Everyone is doing her fair share. And if we're really talking about what's fair, this is the second day in a row you've stayed here so I could go up to the arena, so you're working harder than usual."

"I think we both know that I've been distracted with Stuart's wedding, but I'll make you a deal." Janice rested her hand on Tess's arm. "I'll pay closer attention. Yes, I love my son. I want to be of help to him with this wedding. But his big day is really his to plan, not mine. I do want to give LuAnn the time and space she needs to make her wedding decisions. I think that's important."

"I agree. And even though she's simplifying things for her big day, there are still plans to be made. I want her to feel free to work on that as much as she needs."

"Perfect. So, we'll be a duo—you and me. We'll do what we can to keep things going, even if she gets distracted. And we won't mention it. Agreed?"

Tess nodded. "Agreed. And thank you, Janice. It helps to talk about this. I'm sorry I've let the influx of canines get to me. You always seem to pick up on what I'm feeling. Thank you for that too."

"You're welcome. My internal radar works fine, as long as I pay attention."

Just as they wrapped up their conversation, LuAnn walked into the room. She looked very pretty in her pink floral blouse and white slacks.

Janice whistled and leaned back in her chair and gave LuAnn an admiring look. "Look at you. You're very...springy."

"Thanks." LuAnn's cheeks flushed. "I just felt like dressing up for this breakfast. I guess it's silly, but after traipsing through the mud yesterday I just needed to feel clean and feminine."

"It's not silly at all," Tess said. "I was in the shower for ages last night. I couldn't seem to wash off that smell."

"Me too," LuAnn said. "By the way, that freelance writer is here. I think he's hoping to get some sort of scoop about Jelly's disappearance."

"Ugh." Tess groaned. "Can't we just tell him the Lawsons are sleeping and leave it at that?"

"I did, but he wants to know if he can hang around until they come down. He seems to think they'll head back to the arena this morning, even if Jelly is missing. I wasn't sure how you would feel about that, Janice, since Tess and I are both about to leave. Can he stay?"

Janice shrugged. "Just encourage him to order breakfast at the café. At least he'll be a paying guest, then."

"Good idea," Tess agreed. "I'll do that. But I'm thinking the Lawsons might sleep in, so he could be sitting in there for some time."

"True," Janice agreed. "I haven't heard a sound from the Honeymoon Suite, but that's probably because the kids were up late. It was so sad to hear them crying."

"Yes it was. But don't worry about Winston. I'll take care of him." Tess walked into the lobby and noticed him talking on his phone. He ended the call right away and turned to face her.

She took a few steps in his direction. "Mr. James, we meet again."

"Ah, yes. I believe your name is...Tess?"

"That's right. How did Horace do in his event yesterday?"

Winston offered a sheepish grin. "As well as could be expected for his first time out. He didn't win, but Marigold and I love him, regardless. He's a great friend."

"I'm sorry you lost custody of him." Tess shrugged. "I'm sure that was hard."

"Yeah, me too. You know what they say about a dog being a man's best friend and all." He sighed. "Anyway, I'm wondering if you could point me in the direction of the Lawson family. I was hoping to catch a few minutes with them before they head back to the arena."

"Oh, they haven't come down yet, sorry, and I can't let you go up, because you're not an official guest. I'm sure you understand."

"Right. No sign of the dog, then?"

"Unless they received a call in the night, no."

His brow furrowed. "I can't stop thinking about that groomer."

"What about him?"

"He was surrounded by dogs in crates. I just can't help but wonder if he saw anything. Or…worse."

"Really?" Tess paused to think it through. "He was working, though. Grooming dogs. And he was totally surrounded by people. Besides, he's so high-profile, someone would have noticed."

"Maybe. But you know, there's a history between Russ and the family." Winston gave her a knowing look.

"I just can't imagine he would do something to hurt their dog. Can you?"

Winston shrugged. "You never know with some people. They'll do anything to get back at someone they think has wronged them."

Winnie exited the kitchen with a tray full of muffins. Mr. James took one look at them, and Tess could practically see him salivating.

"Will you be joining us for breakfast in the café?" Tess asked.

"Hmm." He kept his gaze on the muffin tray. "Maybe I will."

He walked into the café and took a seat, then ordered his breakfast. It didn't take long before his food arrived. He ate like a man who might never get another meal. Tess busied herself helping Robin tend to their other customers but kept an eye on Winston's coffee cup to make sure it was filled.

As he wrapped up his meal, Winston gestured for Tess to join him at his table. She walked his direction one more time, coffeepot in hand.

"Would you like one more cup?"

"Please." He leaned back in his chair. "Say, what about the dachshund owner. Is she here?"

"Do you mean Geneva?"

"Yes. I'd love to catch a few minutes with her too. That little dog is a real pistol. I always said she was going to go places."

"Yes, she won Best in Breed yesterday, from what we heard."

"I know. I caught pictures of her in action. Sassy little thing."

"Indeed."

He picked up his cup and nodded. "Thanks for the extra brew. I didn't sleep very well last night."

"There seems to be an epidemic of sleeplessness," Winnie said as she passed by with a fresh tray of muffins. She approached Tess and cleared her throat. "Tess? Could you join me in the kitchen?"

"Sure." Tess followed behind Winnie to the kitchen and headed straight for the sink full of dishes. "What's up, Winnie?"

"I feel like I've seen this guy before, the one you were talking to, I mean."

Tess reached for a dishrag and went to work pre-washing the dishes before putting them into the dishwasher. "He's a freelance writer. I don't think he lives in the area."

"Weird. Maybe he's just got one of those faces."

"Maybe."

She finished up the dishes while Robin and Taylor took over the breakfast crowd. Afterward, Tess grabbed a tube of lipstick from her purse and swiped it over her lips.

"How do I look?" she asked as Robin entered the kitchen with another tray full of dirty dishes in hand.

"Perfect," the young woman exclaimed.

Tess walked out into the parlor at exactly eight ten. The elevator door dinged and then opened. Tess couldn't help but smile when she saw Reena and Richard together inside, looking fresh as daisies. So did the two dogs, for that matter. Schmaltzy and Beauvine were leashed and ready, tails wagging.

Richard gestured with the sweep of a hand for Reena to exit first. She came out with a girlish smile on her face. "We're going to have the best day ever. But first, breakfast. Can the pups stay here, in the parlor? We can hook their leashes under a chair leg, and they'll just sleep. And we can keep an eye on them from the café."

"Of course."

Richard and Reena got the dogs settled next to the sofa, and Tess led the way into the café. Richard followed behind Reena like a lovesick puppy.

Reena pointed to the empty table next to Winston James. Richard pulled out a chair and Reena took a seat, all smiles. She put her hand on her heart, as if overcome. "Oh, Tess, can you believe it? This is the day we'll pass off those precious dogs to their new owners. They'll have forever homes. Just the thought of it makes my heart so happy."

"What's this?" Winston looked their way from his table.

Reena glanced his direction, curiosity in her eyes as she realized the question had come from a total stranger. "Paws on Wheels. It's a rescue organization that transports dogs from shelters in the southern states up north. We're re-homing several dogs today. I'm a Golden Paws member of the organization. Would you be interested in contributing?"

Instead of answering her question, Winston stuck out his hand. "Winston James, freelancer. I write for *Canine Companion*."

Reena shook his hand and gazed at him with intensity. "Reena Newberry. I'm from the Pittsburgh area."

"And you came all this way to help this Paws on Wheels organization?"

"I did. And it's because of my little rescue pup." She pointed at her chiweenie, who had fallen asleep on the parlor floor. "That's my baby over there. Beauvine."

"Bovine? Like cattle?"

She laughed. "Well, sometimes I feel like I'm rounding up cattle when I call for him. He's all over the place."

"Is he a Chiweenie?"

"I'm not a hundred percent sure, but that's the vet's best guess."

"Not a competitor at the big event?"

"Oh, no." Her nose wrinkled. "We don't need ribbons and medals to prove his worth."

Robin dropped off Winston's bill, and he pushed it aside without even looking at it. Tess grabbed the tray with the muffins and another small platter of bacon and carried it to Richard and Reena's table. Then she filled their cups with coffee.

"So tell me more about this Paws on Wheels organization." Winston pulled out his notepad and pen.

"Really?" Her eyes glistened. "Oh, I'd be happy to. It's a fine organization run by a wonderful young man named Jordan Sellers. It has been in existence for a few years. It all started after Hurricane Harvey hit the Houston area, and hundreds of dogs were displaced."

"Wait a minute." Winston snapped his fingers. "This is sounding very familiar. I think I did an interview with this Sellers guy a few years back during the Harvey cleanup. He's from Houston?"

"Yes."

"As I recall there wasn't enough room in the Houston area shelters for all of the dogs, so Jordan and a few of his friends made an appeal to potential dog owners up north. Is that right?"

Reena nodded. "Yes. Before long they found themselves transporting animals hundreds of miles to new owners. And they've kept it up ever since. They make a run every couple of months."

"Interesting. I certainly didn't realize he was still transporting dogs after all this time." He scribbled a few more notes and flipped a page in his notebook. "Who pays for all of this?"

"Supporters like me." She gave him a playful wink. "And you, should you choose to join us. Paws on Wheels is a 501(c)(3), so it's run on donations. But Jordan has put a lot of his own money into it too."

"I wonder if Jordan would be interested in another interview. Maybe the *Canine Companion* would run it this time instead of the local paper. That would be something, wouldn't it?"

"*Something* is the right word." She shrugged. "But I'm not altogether sure that's the best idea, though we do need the promotion. Jordan is a little biased against purebreds, and *Canine Companion* is a publication that caters to purebred owners."

"Oh, I understand. Adopt, don't shop."

"Right." Reena took a sip of her coffee. "Nothing against purebreds, of course."

"Of course," Winston echoed.

Richard took a sip of his coffee, then set the cup down and turned to face Winston. "Did you adopt your dog, Mr. James?"

"Me?" Winston looked dumbfounded by the question.

"Sorry, I thought I overheard you say something earlier at the arena yesterday about your dog competing." Richard pointed to his ears. "My hearing's not what it used to be."

"Oh, yes…Horace. Well, in a manner of speaking. Kind of a long story. I sure do love that big oaf."

Just as they finished breakfast, the Lawson family came down the stairs. Reena rose and took several steps in their direction. She wrapped her arms around Callie. "I heard about your sweet Jelly Bean. I'm so sorry." Her gaze traveled to Andy. "Has there been any word?"

He shook his head. "No. I just placed another call to the police. They've heard nothing."

Winston rose from his spot at the table and approached them. "You've called in the police? I'm sorry to hear it's come to that."

Tandi glanced his way, and concern registered in her eyes as she saw him, along with a hint of recognition.

He extended his hand her way. "Winston James."

She offered him a curt nod. "I remember you, Mr. James. You interviewed us a few years ago when we pulled Jelly from her first competition at the last minute. I believe you did a write-up about the groomer, one that did a bit of damage to his reputation."

"Right, right." His lips curled up in an impish smile. "I'm glad you remember my work."

"Oh yes, we remember." Andy mumbled under his breath, "It would be hard to forget."

Tess showed the family to a table in the café then turned to discover Geneva and Gigi getting off the elevator. They passed right by the café, headed toward the front door. Geneva was in the middle of a heated discussion on her phone. Tess waited until she ended the call and then approached her.

"Are you and Gigi headed back to the arena?"

"We are."

"What's on the agenda today?"

"The agility events. Gigi loves to watch those, and so do I. It will be a lovely distraction."

Tess wanted to ask, "From what?" but didn't.

Geneva gave a little wave and disappeared out the front door.

Richard rose and walked toward the lobby, where he took hold of Schmaltzy's leash. "I'm going to pull up the car so you don't have to walk so far, Reena. I'll be back to fetch you ladies momentarily." He ambled toward the front door, then disappeared outside.

Reena's lips curled upward in a lovely smile, and for the first time Tess noticed her overabundance of makeup. The pink cheeks suited her, but the blue eye shadow was a bit much. Should she tell her?

"Isn't Richard just the sweetest thing?" Reena beamed. "Such a gentleman."

Before Tess could answer, the front door opened, and Brad walked in. He took a couple of steps in her direction as soon as he noticed her. "Tess, perfect. I was hoping to talk to you for a few minutes before I take LuAnn to breakfast."

"Oh?"

"Yes. We've been talking through the wedding plans. I think she's excited about the preparations, but I'm afraid she's also a little disappointed not to get her dream wedding, the one she's planned since she was young. She's decided to go with a simpler plan. I wondered if she was regretting that decision."

Tess paused to think about it. "She hasn't said anything to make me think she's disappointed. I think she's pretty happy about it all. And trust me when I say that we're so busy around here, there's not much time to pull off anything elaborate."

"I understand that." He smiled. "Well, you've made me feel a little better, Tess. I just want her to be happy."

"She is, Brad. In fact, I haven't seen her this happy in years."

"You know I would give her the moon if I could."

"I'm kind of glad you can't. We're pretty crowded in here as it is." Tess chuckled.

At the very moment Janice walked out of the kitchen, LuAnn came bounding down the stairs. She walked a little faster the moment she saw Brad. As she pitched herself into his arms, Tess couldn't help but smile. Seeing her friend this happy did her heart good. If anyone deserved such bliss, LuAnn did.

Janice drew close and whispered, "She only has eyes for Brad. I don't think she's noticed what any of the rest of us are doing."

Tess laughed. "I'm not taking it personally. I think it's wonderful."

"Me too." Janice sighed. "Like a scene from a movie."

As she headed outside with Reena a couple of minutes later, Tess thought about Brad's sweet words, about how much he cared for LuAnn. God was always surpassing the Inn Crowd's wildest imaginations and dreams, and she knew a love like this was something LuAnn had given up hoping for. She was reminded once again that God was caring for all of them, every moment of every day, and in His time, all would be set right, noisy dogs, mistreated dogs, missing dogs, and all.

# CHAPTER NINE

The ride to the arena was entertaining, to say the least. Richard Townsen might be a terrific man and a wonderful dog owner, but his driving skills left something to be desired. Had Tess known what she was in for, she would have opted to take her own vehicle.

Not that anyone else in the car seemed to notice. Reena was too busy swapping stories with Richard about her younger years, and their two dogs were curled up in their respective dog carriers. Tess felt like the odd one out but didn't really mind. In fact, she rather enjoyed listening to the duo in the front seat carry on about where they went to school and what life was like when they were young.

"Are you okay back there, Tess?" Reena asked when there was a break in the conversation. "We're getting a little carried away up here."

"I'm fine. Not sure what I'm in for, so just help me figure that out when we get there, okay?"

"Oh, we'll need all the help we can get. There are over thirty families showing up to give these babies forever homes. We've got to make sure we match the right dog with the right family. It's going to be all hands on deck. Do you mind helping?"

"No, in fact I'd rather be helping than just standing around watching the rest of you work. Just give me something I can manage. That's all I ask."

"I'm sure Jordan will have the perfect job for you. He's so great at figuring out who can do what." Reena carried on, singing Jordan's praises. "And you're going to love his wife, Missy. She's a real peach."

"I think that freelance writer, Winston Something-or-Other, is going to be there today as well," Richard said. "I got the feeling he's a little down on his luck."

"Oh?" Tess was curious about this.

"Yeah, he talked my ear off at the last competition. From what I understand, he used to have a regular column at the *Canine Companion*. He followed the dog shows. But they went through some restructuring and reduced him to a freelance status."

"That's sad," Reena said. "Poor guy."

"Yes. I know he took some heat for his more recent articles, but the older ones were great. I used to look forward to the magazine just so I could read them. He always looked for heroic tales to share."

"Like?" Reena pulled down the visor and slid open the mirror to check her lipstick.

"Like the Australian cattle dog who saved her owner's life by calling 911."

"No way." Reena snapped the mirror shut and flipped the visor back up.

"It's true. The owner had a seizure, and the dog somehow punched in the numbers on the owner's phone. They had trained him to do it."

"Wow. That's nothing short of miraculous," Tess said.

Richard nodded. "Yep. And he did another story about a dog who saved a child from drowning."

"All of these were show dogs?" Tess asked.

"Yes. Not necessarily dogs who did well in the ring, mind you, but competitors, nonetheless."

"Great human interest angle." Tess's admiration for the man went up as she pondered the tales he'd shared.

*Tales. Tails. Funny.*

Richard carried on, oblivious to Tess's internal laughter. "I remember one article he did about an elderly owner who lost her spouse. Her dog saved her life when she went into a diabetic coma. Such a fascinating story."

"He really does look for the heart tuggers, sounds like," Tess acknowledged.

"Always has. He just has a knack for snooping out those kinds of stories."

"And now the *Canine Companion* doesn't print his stuff?"

"I think he sells his articles to local papers and smaller publications now. I'm not sure. But I miss those old articles. They were great. I tell you what. I'm going to look up that 911 article so you can read it for yourself. It's really fascinating to think that a dog could be trained to make a phone call."

"No kidding."

Richard went into a sneezing fit. He got so distracted that he missed the turn into the arena parking lot. He slammed on his brakes and put his car into REVERSE, then managed a very sharp jerk to the left. Before long they were parked in a spot near the Paws on Wheels van. Tess wasn't sure she'd be able to get out of her door, with the car being parked at such an odd angle, but she would do her best.

"Wow, lots of cars here today," she observed as she reached for her purse.

"The competition is still going on," Richard explained. "Agility rounds."

"Oh, that's right. Geneva told me about that."

"Maybe when we're done getting all of the babies into the arms of their new owners we can go over and sneak a peek at the pups running through their courses," Richard suggested. "How would that be? Then maybe we could get some lunch."

For the first time it occurred to Tess that she might actually be stuck with these two all day long. Why, oh why, hadn't she brought her own car? She eased the car door open and managed to squeeze out without bumping the door into the truck next to them. Not that anyone noticed. Reena and Richard were too busy getting their babies out of their carriers and then leashing them up.

Tess glanced toward the Paws on Wheels bus and noticed a line of people standing outside.

"Wow." A quick glance at her watch revealed the time— 8:31. "They're early."

Reena patted her on the arm. "Honey, when you've waited for a new baby and know it's delivery day, you make a point to be early."

"Looks like it." Tess shifted her position and slung her purse over her shoulder. On second thought, maybe she'd better leave it in the car.

"Richard, would you mind if I put my purse in the trunk? I don't want to risk losing it."

"Don't mind a bit." He popped the trunk, and she deposited her purse.

They made the trek to the bus, where Jordan met them with a smile. He introduced his wife, Missy, and a trio of other volunteers, Norah, Jamie, and Chip.

Jordan looked delighted to see her. "I can't thank you enough for coming, Tess. This is a great surprise. We need all the help we can get."

"I'm happy to help. Just show me where to go and what to do."

"I will, as soon as I figure it out."

"Is the film crew here yet?" Reena looked around as she fussed with her hair. "I'm ready for my close-up."

Jordan laughed. "Yes, they're here. Mack is already inside the bus getting some footage of the dogs." He yawned. "You wouldn't believe what a long night we had."

"We didn't get much sleep, just leave it at that." Missy faced Reena and sighed. "You know Prissy?"

"The little poodle mix?" Reena laughed. "Boy, do I ever. Yappy little thing."

"Well, she kept us up all night. After we fed and walked her, she didn't want to go back into the crate. She just wanted to be held. I kept trying to fall asleep with her in my lap, but neither of us got much rest."

"You guys sleep on the bus?" Tess asked.

"Sure. We've got a mattress we pull down at night. Jordan and I manage okay, but we can't bring other workers with us from Texas. That's why we're so grateful to have our Marietta team ready to roll. And now that team includes you, Tess!"

"Happy to be here." For the first time it occurred to Tess that Jordan and his wife really were willing to sacrifice anything, even their own comfort, for the dogs.

She could hear the pups barking from inside the bus.

Several more adopters walked up to the check-in table, but no one was there to greet them.

"I'll tell you what, Tess—since you haven't had experience handling the dogs before, I think I'll put you at the table."

"What will I do?"

"I'll have the new owners line up by number. Each of them should have the paperwork they filled out online—the adoption form and the forty-dollar adoption fee, which covers the cost of the shots and other veterinary expenses."

Richard shook his head. "My goodness. You sure don't make any money, do you?"

"Well, we're a nonprofit, remember." Jordan turned back to Tess. "When they get to the table you'll match their paperwork with the outtake forms I'll give you. Everything is stapled together and kept for our records, except for the receipt for the forty dollars, which you'll give to the new owner. Just make sure the dog's ID number is on the receipt. Got it?"

"Um, I think." She laughed.

"Don't worry, Tess. I'll be there to help you." Richard gave her a smile. "We'll make a good team."

Missy rested her hand on Tess's arm. "Let's go inside, and I'll introduce you to the others. That way you'll know who's who. Oh, and I'll give you a Paws on Wheels T-Shirt to put on. There's a bathroom on the bus. You can change in there."

"Okay…" Tess followed Missy, Jordan, and Reena into the bus. Once inside, her eyes took a moment to adjust. Then she saw crates and crates of dogs, all eager to find their freedom. A tiny little Yorkie mix peered at her from behind the wire front of her cage. "Hello there, sweetheart," she said. No sooner had the words escaped than she realized the film crew probably caught it on tape. "Oops." She smiled at the cameraman and shrugged.

"It's okay," he said. "We've got all we need for now. We're headed outside to interview families and film the adoptions as they take place. I'm Mack, by the way."

"Nice to meet you, Mack." She offered him a warm smile then turned back to the dogs.

Mack had a couple of questions for Jordan, and then he and his crew exited the bus. Jordan handed a T-shirt to Tess, and she went into the tiny bathroom to change.

When she emerged, Jordan's face beamed. "Now you're really one of the team."

Just as quickly, Jordan's smile faded. Tess followed his gaze and realized that Winston had arrived.

"Not that guy again." Jordan muttered under his breath. "I thought I shook him years ago."

"Is there a problem with Winston?" Tess asked.

Jordan started to say something but must have thought better of it. He shrugged and said, "It'll be okay," then dropped it.

He quickly called the team together to give instructions, and everyone gathered in front of the bus to hear what he had to say, including Winston, who took copious notes.

"Chip and I will take the dogs out of the crates in order of their ID numbers. Missy will call out the numbers on the megaphone, and the new owners will step forward to the table with paperwork in hand. Norah, you stand at the door of the bus, and I'll pass the dogs to you. You can go with the owners to the table, where Tess and Richard will handle the paperwork and give receipts. We'll only handle a couple of dogs at a time, but that's okay. We're not in any hurry." He pointed to Mack and his team. They were busy filming the line of adopters. "Reena, you and Beauvine work the crowd. Visit with the people while they're waiting. Tell them about us—what we do, how we do it—that sort of thing. Tell them your story about adopting Beauvine and how grateful you are that you adopted instead of shopping for a purebred. And remember, we'll have a lot of people stop by just because they're curious. Visit with them as well. Try to get them on board as sponsors. If and when the local newspapers or news stations show up, please come and get me."

"Aye aye, Cap'n!" She saluted him.

"Okay, let's all take our places, then." He gave his crew a grateful smile. "And in case I haven't already said this ten thousand times, thank you all for doing what you do. It's a very good thing, and we certainly couldn't manage without you."

Tess's heart swelled with pride. Well, pride mixed with nerves. The idea of handling so much paperwork seemed a little daunting. She took her seat at the table next to Richard. He gestured for Schmaltzy to lie down on the ground next to his feet.

At exactly nine o'clock, Jordan grabbed a megaphone and made an announcement for the people to line up according to the dogs' ID numbers. It took a bit of shuffling, but before long the families were in a single line down the sidewalk.

Winston pulled out his notebook and pen and approached Jordan with a couple of rapid-fire questions.

Jordan put his hand up. "Sorry, but I don't have time to talk right now. Catch me later."

Something was definitely amiss between those two. She would have to ask Reena about it later, once things settled down.

Winston turned his attention to Missy. He tried to distract her with his queries, but she offered a firm response as well. "I'll answer any questions you have after we're through. These folks have waited a long time for this day, and I need to stay focused on them."

He seemed surprised by her curt response but stepped back. "Got it."

"Everyone ready?" Jordan called out from the bus.

"Ready," they responded in unison.

The dogs all began to bark, which was a little disconcerting, but Tess couldn't really blame them. There was an excitement in the air that gave the place a sense of wonder and joy.

Jordan reached inside the first crate and came out with a little black-and-white terrier mix. From the paperwork in front of her, Tess could see that the dog's name was Luna. Missy called out the dog's name and ID number and the new owner—a woman with jet-black hair—stepped forward toward the table. Norah carried the little dog to her new owner and placed her in her arms. The little pooch's tail wagged and wagged.

"Oh. My. Goodness." The woman's eyes filled with tears. "Don't you just love her? I've been staring at her picture for over a week, anticipating this day. And now, here she is. Isn't she just the sweetest?" She tipped the dog back to look into her face. "Just you wait till you get to your new home, Luna. You've got a new dog bed, and some toys and yummy treats. And you're just going to love your big brother, Buddy!"

"Oh, you have a son?" Richard asked. "That's perfect!"

"No." The woman laughed. "I have a beagle mix named Buddy. He's six years old and in desperate need of a friend. I think these two are going to get along just fine."

"Perfect." Tess managed the paperwork with no problem at all. Good thing too, because another dog arrived directly on the heels of that one, a Chihuahua named Butch.

"What a sweet little pup," Tess said. "I can't believe he was overlooked in a shelter."

His new owner, a young man covered in tattoos, handed off the paperwork. "There's a reason for that. When he was brought into the shelter he had the worst case of mange they had ever seen. He was also a Parvo pup, and many of them don't make it. In fact, he's the only one in his litter who did. So, he's a special little guy."

"He's healthy now, though, right?"

"He is, but it took two months and hundreds of dollars worth of treatments to get him there. Shelters don't have the money to cover those costs, which is why a lot of these dogs are euthanized when their case seems hopeless. Butch here was one of the lucky ones. Or maybe I should say I'm the lucky one. I've been following his story online for weeks, but I finally get to take him home with me." He leaned in close and whispered, "I think this little fella will give me a new lease on life."

Tess took care of Butch's paperwork and handed the man his receipt. After Butch came a pointer mix and then some sort of poodle-thing. The dog following the poodle was adorable, but Tess couldn't make out the breed.

"Oh my goodness!" she said to Norah. "What *is* this precious little thing with the scrunchy face?"

Norah handed the dog to her new owner, a well-dressed woman with an expensive purse, and turned to face Tess. "Kiki, here? She's a French bulldog mix. Not sure what she's mixed with."

The feisty pup squirmed in her new owner's arms, and the woman burst into tears. She planted kisses on the dog's head and carried on about how she'd been praying for her for days.

Next came a beautiful black dog named Trigger, bigger than the little boy proclaiming him his new best friend.

"Lab mix?" Richard asked as he helped Tess with the paperwork.

"Lab mix." The little boy's father patted the dog on the head. "I think there's a little Husky mixed in."

"So he's going to be a big dog."

"Hard to tell the breed sometimes," Norah explained to the new owner. "But if you ever really want to know Trigger's history, you can always order a DNA test."

"You can test a dog's DNA?" Tess asked as she stapled pages together. "Really?"

"Yes, it's a fascinating process," Norah explained. "People with mixed-breed dogs can get their questions answered with a simple test. Not that it really matters, but some folks like to know, just out of curiosity."

"And because some breeds have particular health issues," Richard added.

Wow. Tess was learning a lot today.

She kept the line moving as quickly as possible. The dogs came in all shapes and sizes—terriers, spaniels, and pit bulls.

"Pitties are the hardest to place," Norah explained as she brought a gorgeous big dog to its new owner. "So many apartment complexes and rental homes won't allow them because they're considered to be dangerous dogs. Thumbelina here is lucky to have a new home."

"Thumbelina?" Tess had to fight to keep from laughing out loud at that name.

"Don't you just love it?" The new owner, a petite woman, nuzzled up to her new dog, and the pit bull licked her arm. "I guess you can see how vicious she is." She laughed. "The only thing I'm going to have to watch out for is slobber. But to be honest, I could use a little love right now, even if it's messy." The sadness in her eyes pricked Tess's heart, but she didn't ask any questions. She took care of Thumbelina's paperwork and handed the receipt to the woman, who was all smiles.

After about an hour a reporter from the local news station appeared with a small film crew. They peppered the new dog owners with questions and then turned their attention to Jordan, who was happy to give an interview. When they finished, a reporter from the *Marietta Times* stopped by, also loaded with questions. He scribbled his notes into a notebook, much like the one Winston carried. Tess looked on as Jordan and Missy handled all of the incoming media folks with ease. No doubt they were accustomed to the press.

Tess kept on working until the line grew shorter and shorter. She met so many amazing people—and dogs—along the way. The adorable little Sheltie mix had the softest fur of the bunch. And talk about friendly! The wiggly little thing could hardly wait to start kissing her new family, a mom and dad with four children. As the family waited, the kids carried on about how excited they were to be getting their new pet.

Tess was touched by the joy she witnessed from a single mom with two teenagers when they met their Irish setter mix, Scarlet. The dog was magnificent—a lovely reddish-brown.

Out of the corner of her eye, Tess caught a glimpse of Winston asking questions of a woman in the line. The woman approached Tess at the table when her Maltese mix was brought out.

"Oh, you're here at last!" She gave the little pooch several kisses, then attached his new collar and leash while Tess worked on the papers. The woman set the dog down, and he began to sniff her shoes and then her ankles. "I think he smells my cat." She laughed. "I sure hope they get along."

"Penny's great with cats," Jordan called out from the bus.

"How does he know that?" the woman asked. "There aren't any cats on board, right?"

"Oh, trust me, he knows everything about our dogs before they're ever transported," Norah explained. "He really takes his time to get to know and love every animal before and during the transport."

"Remarkable." The woman sauntered off with her new pup at her heels.

Soon the line was down to just one person, a man in a wheelchair with a full beard and mustache. He wore a cap with the words *Semper Fi.* That wasn't what drew Tess's attention, though. She couldn't help but notice that the man was missing the bottom half of his right leg. She turned her gaze, not wanting to appear rude.

Reena approached the table and pulled up a chair as the man waited for his dog to appear. "I'm pooped," she said.

"I'll bet you are." Richard gave her an admiring smile. "You've been on your feet all morning."

"It's for a good cause." She turned as Jordan hand-delivered the man's dog, a little Jack Russel terrier mix. Reena released a little squeal as she saw the pup. "Oh, look! It's Tripod! I met him yesterday. He's a doll."

"How does he manage on only three legs?" Tess asked as she picked up the final stack of papers.

"Simple," Jordan chimed in. "He doesn't realize there's one missing. It's normal for him."

Tess finished up the paperwork then leaned back in her chair, exhausted but exhilarated.

"Job well done, team." Jordan beamed with pride. "There's no way we could have done this without you."

The cameraman approached Jordan. He glanced down at his notebook and then back up again. "We got footage from all of the families. They were great, by the way." He turned to face Reena. "And you've got a superstar in this one. She was fantastic—with the kids and the dogs. Everyone loved her."

Reena beamed. "I shall become the national spokesperson for Paws on Wheels. Just call me Reena the Rescuer!"

"Reena the Rescuer." Jordan chuckled. "That's a great idea." He slipped his arm around her shoulder. "I'm so grateful for you, Reena. You've been like a ray of sunshine on this bus. You're not just a generous benefactor, you're a blessing to all of us."

"She's also a savvy businesswoman with a lot of pull." These words came from Richard. "She's managed to talk many of the people she's met into giving monthly donations. I say you put her to work in the booth inside the dog show. Set up some sort of incentive for people to give donations."

"That's a great idea."

"I'm happy to be of service." Reena beamed. "Put me to work, friends."

"She has more energy than all the rest of us put together," Tess admitted. "This has been wonderful, but I'm beat."

She glanced up and saw a poster on the side of the bus, one she hadn't noticed before. In it, a little boy lay on the ground on his tummy, face-to-face with a giant yellow lab. The two were nose to nose. The caption underneath the picture read, "Who's rescuing who?"

Her heart caught in her throat as she thought about how she'd witnessed that very thing today. These people had come to rescue dogs who'd made it through life's storms, but many of them had weathered storms of their own. Their stories had tugged at her heart.

"I think I'm starting to see how much these dogs mean to their owners," Tess said. "Is it awful that I didn't get it until now?"

"Not awful at all." Reena reached down and picked up Beauvine, then held him close. "They're such a comfort to us when we're going through bad times. I honestly don't know what I'll do when it's Beauvine's time to…" She shook her head. "Anyway, let's just pray he outlives me, because I'd be lost without him."

Tess stopped to think about that. So many elderly people lived alone with only the companionship of their pets. Wasn't it wonderful of the Lord to create them?

"Winnie told Janice earlier today that she was peopled out," Tess confessed. "And to be honest, I've been feeling the same way. I didn't know how many more people I could take this week. This process was exhausting but really touching as well."

"It feels good, doesn't it?" Reena rested a hand on Tess's arm. "But just for the record, I get peopled out sometimes too. I love being at home, in my own space. I think everyone feels that way." She cuddled Beauvine. "Of course, I couldn't imagine my home without my little lovebug here. I'm sure you feel the same way about Huck."

"Right." Tess nodded. Suddenly, in that very moment, she did.

She wanted to revel in this excitement, but something caught her eye. Winston was trailing after the petite woman with the pit bull, drilling her with questions. His pushiness made Tess uncomfortable. She could tell the woman was uncomfortable too. Still, it wasn't her place to intervene, was it?

## CHAPTER TEN

*April 4ᵗʰ, 1862*

Throughout the night, Prudence heard the dog whimpering. No amount of shushing worked. Jason finally rose from the bed and went to sit in the chair at the table. The dog joined him. It wasn't long before Prudence gave up and wandered into the kitchen as well. She prepared the morning coffee—they were going to need plenty of it—and fixed a cup for Jason.

"I think he is lonely." Jason stroked the mastiff's head, and the dog calmed at once. "Poor thing."

"Likely missing his owner, Alex." Prudence felt her heart lurch. "How sad, to come so far, only to lose the one thee loves the most."

Her heart was pricked, even as she spoke the words. For while she felt safe in the farmhouse with Jason, she couldn't imagine how she would go on if she ever lost him. Tears sprang to her eyes at the very idea. She brushed them away and fixed herself a cup of coffee.

In so many ways, she felt for the dog. He came from the South but somehow ended up on the Union side. Was he mourning not just the loss of his friend Alex, but a former Confederate master as well? Was that man kind to him or a cruel and heartless master?

Her thoughts shifted to the many slaves who had traveled through the hotel on their way north. Like the dog, they all had masters. Many, if not most, came from situations where they had been treated unkindly. Perhaps even the dog who sat at the master's feet was treated with more regard.

How many had passed through the hotel over the months? In all that time, she'd never once encountered a dog. And now, here he sat, her guest of honor.

"Here, boy." She clucked her tongue, and Jack walked her way. She glanced down at the cloth she'd wrapped around his leg and realized it would need to be changed soon.

Prudence stroked his head and gazed into his big brown eyes. "I want thee to know that thee is still loved, even though thy master is gone now. And thee will have a home where people care about thee. Just hold on until thee gets there. I will try to get Nate all fixed up if thee promises to behave thyself while I do." She placed her hand under the dog's chin and lifted his face. "Is that a promise, then?"

"If I did not know any better, I would say thee was smitten with that dog." Jason's eyes twinkled with merriment.

"This one is special. I just felt like he needed to be reminded that he matters, even now."

"Even now?"

"Now that his master is gone, and his work on the battle-field is behind him. Even now, he has value."

"Ah." Jason gave her a curious look. "Is thee sure we are just talking about the dog here?"

"What does thee mean?"

"Pru..." He took a sip of his coffee and then set the mug on the table. "Thee is the hardest worker I know. Thee gives and gives and then gives even more. Thy life is like a bottle of oil poured out for people who come through town in need of help. And I know thee. Thee would be the first to get in line if someone asked for volunteers to care for the downtrodden."

She shrugged. "I am a hard worker. No doubt about it."

"Thy work is for others. And I hope and pray there will come a day when thee can rest easy. Get off of thy feet. Put that broom of thine away and stop fretting over who is coming and who is going in the tunnels below your feet."

Her eyes filled with tears. "Jason, until this war is behind us, I do not see how that will happen. Thee knows God has called me to this." She sniffled. "And besides, I am not ready to be put out to pasture just yet."

"Of course not. I know thee, Pru." He slipped his arm over her shoulder and pulled her close. "Thee will go right on working, even when thee is old and gray."

"And thee will love me, wrinkles and all?"

He planted a kiss in her hair and whispered, "Like a pup loves his master."

# CHAPTER ELEVEN

Tess kept her gaze on the woman with the pit bull as Winston continued to drill her with questions.

Jordan must have noticed too. He glanced that direction. "What is Winston James up to now?"

"I don't know, but it's pretty obvious from her body language that she's uncomfortable around him."

"I'll take care of it. I've already learned the hard way that he's not a man to be trusted. But I'll be the bigger person." Jordan called out to Winston, "Hey, Mr. James, if you're ready for a tour of the inside of the bus, this is the time."

Winston stopped his conversation with the woman and turned their way. "Really? That's awesome."

"Yes, but we need to hurry. My crew wants to leave to get lunch soon."

"I'll be fast as lightning." Winston gave the woman a shrug and sprinted in Jordan's direction.

The woman approached Tess. She held tight to the pit bull's leash with one hand and put the other hand over her heart. "Please thank Jordan for me, will you? I don't know what that reporter wanted, but I couldn't seem to shake him. I guess Thumbelina wasn't the only one who needed rescuing today."

"I'm sure he's harmless, but I could tell you were uncomfortable."

She nodded, eyes wide. "I was, and I didn't want him to see which car I was getting into. Is that weird?" She looked around, as if expecting him to reappear.

"Not weird at all. A girl can't be too safe these days."

"I guess." The young woman rose and took a few steps toward a light blue SUV. She opened the door and ushered the dog inside, then thanked Tess once again.

Tess waited until the vehicle pulled away then turned around to walk back to the bus. When she got there, she found Jordan and Winston emerging.

"Thanks for the tour, Jordan." Winston gave him a nod. "Great job today. Thanks for letting me hang out so I could catch the story."

"Anything we can do to promote the organization," Jordan responded.

Winston lifted his notebook in the air and headed toward the arena.

"Thank you." Tess tilted her head toward Winston's retreating back. "I could tell he was making that woman uncomfortable."

"I picked up on it too." Jordan sighed. "He's got a long history of making people uncomfortable, me included. But on a day like today I was feeling generous, so I invited him on board. And who knows? Maybe this time he'll put together a great article to promote the organization. It could happen."

"I hope so. What you guys are doing here is great, Jordan."

"Thanks." Jordan smiled. "And speaking of that, thank you again for helping out today."

"My pleasure."

"We're going to grab a quick bite and then come back to man the booth inside the arena. Care to join us?"

"I'd love to."

She fell in step with him as they walked back toward the bus. From inside, she distinctly heard the sound of a dog barking.

"Did we forget one?" Tess asked.

"No." Missy shook her head. "We took in a local dog yesterday afternoon, an emergency case. We're hanging on to her until a home can be found. But I don't mind. I've gotten rather attached to this one, honestly."

"Oh." Tess walked over to the table and picked up the stack of papers she'd gathered all morning. She handed them to Missy with a smile. "Thanks again for letting me help. It felt really good."

"See?" Reena slipped her arm around Tess's waist and gave her a hug. "I knew you would love it."

"I knew it too." Richard eased his way up from his chair at the table. He roused Schmaltzy from his slumber, then reached for the dog's leash. "Dogs have a way of nosing their way into our hearts before we realize it."

"This whole thing makes me feel even worse for the Lawson family." As Tess spoke the words, her heart felt pricked. "They love Jelly like one of their own children. I'm sure their hearts are broken."

From inside the bus, the dog started barking once again. Jordan's gaze shifted toward the bus, and he took a couple of steps in that direction, then said, "I'll check on our last remaining passenger and be right back. You guys decide where we'll go to lunch."

They put their heads together and settled on Over the Moon just up the street. Minutes later, Richard was behind the wheel with Reena in the passenger seat and Tess in the back.

"This is just how the day started," Tess observed. "But so much has happened in such a short time." She paused and thought through the morning's events. "You know, I'm fond of dogs, but I haven't had one tug on my heart the way Beauvine and Schmaltzy have tugged on yours in a long time. But today I really saw what a difference a new home could make—not just to the dogs but to the owners. Did you see that one woman, the one who lost her husband three months ago?"

"Mrs. Smalley?" Richard asked.

"Yes. That little dachsie is going to be just the ticket." Tess's eyes filled with tears as the memory flooded over her. "I honestly think the dog will be as good for her as she will be for the dog."

"Well, of course, honey." Reena glanced back at her with a smile. "That's exactly what it's been like with Beauvine too. I was such a homebody before, always feeling sorry for myself.

Having him has forced me to get out and take walks, to meet people, to get involved in things."

"My favorite adoption was the fellow who took Tripod." Richard cleared his throat. "When I realized that the pup's new owner was a disabled veteran, it took everything inside of me not to burst into tears." He sighed. "I guess it wouldn't be very manly to cry, but I almost did."

"Cry all you like," Reena said. "I know I did. God bless that veteran for taking on a pup like Tripod."

"If anyone could understand, he could. It's almost as if..." he paused.

"They belonged together." Tess finished the sentence for him.

"Yes, that's it. It's like God brought them together so they could complete one another." Richard's words were directed at Tess, but his gaze was solidly fixed on Reena.

For a moment, a peaceful silence grew. Tess began to fidget with her phone, to look busy. Reena finally took the hint. "Let's get to that pizza place, shall we? I'm starving."

They met up with Jordan, Missy, Norah, Jamie, and Chip at Over the Moon Pizza and had a quick lunch. Tess had a wonderful time listening to Jordan share some of the adventures he and Missy experienced on the drive up to Ohio from Texas. Afterward, he shared his vision for the organization, and before the lunch was over, Tess had committed to become a Golden Paws sponsor. She wasn't quite sure how he did it, but Jordan had a way of making people feel passionate about his cause.

As they were wrapping up their lunch, her cell phone rang. She glanced down and saw LuAnn's number, then answered with a quiet, "Hello?"

"Hey, you. Why so hush-hush?"

"I'm at Over the Moon having lunch with Reena and her crew. They're having a very passionate conversation about puppy training. I hate to interrupt."

"Funny. Did they talk you into taking one of the dogs from the bus?"

"No." Tess laughed. "But the dogs I met today were pretty amazing. I wish you could've heard some of their stories."

"I figured you'd fall head over heels, Tess. I know I would have. I'm not sure I could have walked away without one, myself."

"They were all spoken for." Tess paused to think about the lone dog still crated on the bus. "Well, most of them, anyway. There's one left on the bus."

"Don't even think about it."

Tess laughed. "I won't. If I showed up at the inn with a second dog, Janice would probably kill me."

"Probably."

"Hey, how did your breakfast with Brad go? Have you started making wedding plans?"

"Nothing solid. But we had a great time. I'm back at the inn now. Things are kind of slow around here. Janice took off to meet Zelda at the craft store, and this place is a little too quiet for me. Winnie's going to be here baking for the next couple of hours, and I thought I might sneak away to the arena to watch a couple of the agility rounds. Brad said they're a lot of fun."

"Sounds good. Maybe you could take me back to the inn if Reena stays to work in the Paws on Wheels booth."

"Happy to. We can figure all of that out when I get there."

"Great. We're headed back to the arena in a few minutes. I'll meet you in the grooming area."

"Why the grooming area?" LuAnn asked.

"I'm still bugged by how Jelly managed to slip by so many people in that area yesterday. Maybe if I get another visual it will trigger some sort of idea. I don't know."

"Okay, see you there."

Tess ended the call and turned her attention back to the others at the table.

"Everything okay?" Missy asked.

"Yes, that was my friend LuAnn. She's headed up to the arena to watch the agility rounds. I told her I'd meet her there."

"We'd better hit the road, then." Missy eased herself out of the booth, and Jordan followed. It turned out Richard had already secretly paid the bill. She could tell from the look of pleasure in his eyes that he enjoyed treating others.

Before long they were all headed back to the arena. When they arrived, Tess parted ways with Richard and Reena, who had decided to cover the Paws on Wheels booth as a team. Tess walked through the crowd to the grooming area. She stood back at a distance, observing Russ Schumer clip a fancy poodle. The man really did know how to get the job done.

She happened to catch a glimpse of Andy Lawson walking toward the family lounge. He noticed her and took several steps in her direction.

"Any word on—"

Tess couldn't even get the words out before he shook his head. "No. Nothing. We've made the rounds again and no one has seen her since yesterday after her event. I just decided to swing back by the grooming area to talk to some of the groomers. I want to ask them if they remember seeing anything yesterday. I mean, the whole thing happened right here, after all."

"I'll come with you. If you're okay with that, I mean. It's been impossible for me to think that no one saw a thing."

"Agreed." He pointed to a young woman covered in tattoos who was working on a large Afghan hound. "Let's start with her. Her name is Charity."

They approached the woman, and Tess couldn't help but stand in awe as the dog was transformed before her very eyes. The once-hairy beast was now a work of art.

"That's remarkable," she said after watching for a few moments.

"Thanks. My work is very gratifying." Charity shifted her gaze in Tess and Andy's direction and smiled. "I love what I do."

"And it shows," Andy said. "You're great at it."

"Thanks." She shrugged and continued her work. "I might not be a superstar groomer, but I get the job done. Haven't had any complaints yet."

Was Tess imagining it, or did Charity cast a bitter gaze in Russ Schumer's direction as she spoke?

Charity mumbled something under her breath. Tess couldn't make out most of it but did manage to hear Russ's name.

"You know Russ Schumer?" Andy asked.

The groomer continued her work on the hound, now focusing on his right front leg. "You could say that. I used to work for him."

"You did?" Tess was intrigued by this revelation. "Wow. I hear he's the best."

"Thanks a lot." Charity rolled her eyes then went back to work on the Afghan, who had taken to fidgeting.

"Oh, I didn't mean..." Tess paused and thought through her next words. "I'm just going by what people say."

"People say what they're taught to say. When all you hear is how amazing one person is, you begin to believe it."

Andy cleared his throat. "Listen, I hate to disturb you, but my dog Angelica went missing yesterday afternoon."

Charity's mouth dropped open as she gazed at him. "You're the one who lost your dog? I was so sorry to hear about that. You still haven't found her?"

"No." He shook his head. "It's like she disappeared right into thin air."

"Hardly. An award-winning spaniel like that? She was stolen. No doubt about it." Charity went back to work on the Afghan. "I'd bet a year's salary on it." She paused and nodded in Russ's direction. "My salary, not his."

"Were you here yesterday when it happened?" Andy asked.

"I was in the far corner, working." She pointed to a spot on the east side of the room. "Most of the others have shuffled in and out along the edges. If I'm being honest—and what would be the point of lying?—yesterday was all about Russ. He was given plenty of space to work, and right in the center of the room, where the cameras could get the best shots of him. The rest of us did our best to fade into the background so he could get the accolades he wanted."

"But why?" Tess asked. "Why does everyone cater to him?"

"He's like a Hollywood star, I guess. Even *you* seemed to think so, remember?"

"Oh, I…" Tess's words drifted off, and she decided to change gears. "So, the rest of you were in and out, which means that Russ was the only groomer who was here the whole time?"

"I noticed that he took off at one point to deal with one of the dogs who was crated, but other than that he was right there, at his station." She gestured with her head. "Doing what he does best, drawing a crowd. You should probably talk to him. He loves it when people fawn over him."

Andy squared his shoulders. "I'll talk to him, but there won't be any fawning. Tess, are you coming with me?"

"You go ahead. I'll be there in a minute." She wanted to stick around to ask this woman a couple more questions. Once Andy was out of earshot, she said, "Tell me more about Russ. I mean, you worked for him, and it's clear you're not his biggest fan. What kind of person is he?"

"You mean, what kind of *person* or what kind of *groomer*?"

"Either…or both. I'm curious to know what he does when he's not grooming dogs."

"Hmm." Charity wrinkled her nose. "If you want to know all of that, you should ask that writer guy. The one who used to work for the *Canine Companion*. He was just over here a little while ago, asking all these same questions."

"Oh?"

"Yeah, I don't know why everyone's so interested in Russ. I mean, he's a great groomer, but there are others in the business too, you know. One of these days those magazines are going to realize that."

Tess didn't get a chance to question Charity further, because the Afghan's owner returned. Oh well. Tess turned and took several steps away from her. Before she made it very far, LuAnn walked up.

"Hey there, I've been looking for you." She brushed a loose strand of hair out of her face. "Who was that I saw you talking to?"

"One of the groomers. I don't think she's a big fan of Russ's."

"Why is that?"

"She used to work for him," Tess explained. "I got the feeling he didn't treat her very well. I've heard from others that he's very temperamental."

"I'd be temperamental too if someone wrote an ugly article about me, especially one that twisted the truth."

"Yeah."

"I'm sorry it took me so long to get here, but I stopped off at the Paws on Wheels booth to visit with Reena and Richard." LuAnn pointed behind her, and Tess noticed Richard standing there. He walked their way, all smiles.

"Did you get bored helping Reena?" Tess asked.

"No, just a little antsy. Schmaltzy wanted to go for a walk." He pointed down, and Tess realized he'd brought the dog with him. "This little fellow spent the morning lounging under our table, and now he's raring to go. It was a pipe dream to think he'd be still in that booth. He's got other plans, trust me." Richard leaned down and scooped the dog up. "Maybe this will calm him down."

"Maybe." Out of the corner of her eye, Tess caught a glimpse of Andy, who was approaching Russ's grooming station. "If you'll excuse me, I need to chat with Andy."

"No worries," Richard said. "I might tag along with you, if you don't mind."

"I don't mind a bit."

Tess, LuAnn, and Richard caught up to Andy just as Russ wrapped up the grooming job on the French poodle.

"Great job! He looks amazing," Tess said to break the ice.

"Thank you." Russ swung around to face her, a broad smile on his face. When he caught a glimpse of Andy standing next to her, the smile faded. Just as quickly, he seemed to notice Richard, and the edges of his lips tilted back upward. He glanced down at Schmaltzy, and his eyes brightened. "Well now, here's that handsome fellow I worked on yesterday." Russ knelt down and scratched the dog behind the ears. "I heard you took third place. Good job, Schmaltzy."

"With a cut from Russ Schumer, he should have taken first." Richard beamed. "But I don't place any stock in ribbons or medals. I'm just in this for the fun."

"Then you're a rarity." Russ turned his attention back to the poodle.

"A rarity." Richard chuckled. "I guess I am." He shifted his gaze to Schmaltzy. "I hate to cut this short, folks, but this little guy needs to go outside, and then we need to get back to the Paws on Wheels booth. I'm sure Reena is missing me."

Was it Tess's imagination, or did Richard's cheeks turn pink the moment he mentioned Reena's name?

He took off through the crowd, and Tess turned her attention back to Russ. She and the others watched in silence as he worked. After a few moments he turned their way.

"I get the feeling you're more than just casual observers. How can I help you folks?"

Andy cleared his throat. "Russ, I wondered if I could ask you a couple of questions. I don't know if you heard, but my dog Angelica went missing yesterday."

"Yes, I heard." Russ continued to brush the poodle. "I was so sorry to hear that."

"I was wondering if you saw—or heard—anything." Andy pointed to the area just past where they were standing. "My wife was right there, where the grooming station meets up with the family lounge. Jelly was in her crate resting while my wife visited with a friend."

"As you know, my station is always busy. I don't have time to babysit anyone's dog." The dog brush slipped out of Russ's hand and landed on the table.

"Of course not. I just wondered if you happened to notice anything odd yesterday afternoon, that's all."

Russ turned and put his hands on his hips. "If I told you all of the odd things I've seen and heard since I arrived at this arena we'd be here all day. I can promise you, I did not see anyone waltz out of here with your dog, Mr. Lawson. And if you're in any way trying to bring some sort of accusation against me like you did before—"

"No!" Andy put his hand up. "I can assure you, I'm not. And for the record, despite what that reporter said in his article, I've never had any animosity toward you, Russ. Ever."

Russ's tension seemed to ease a little at that proclamation. He picked up the brush and started going over the poodle once again. "Well, as I said, I've seen a lot of strange things but didn't notice anyone take your dog. I would tell you if I had."

"Thank you." Andy gave him a polite nod and then walked toward the family lounge. Tess and LuAnn tagged along behind him.

He collapsed in the nearest chair and glanced up at Tess and LuAnn. "Oh, I'm sorry! I should have offered one of you ladies the seat."

He rose, but Tess gestured for him to sit back down.

"I think you need to rest a minute," she said. "You've been through a lot over the past twenty-four hours."

"You certainly didn't deserve that kind of treatment. That fellow needs an attitude adjustment." LuAnn looked Russ's way and grimaced. "Was it just me, or did he seem like he had his nose out of joint?"

"He's obviously still angry at us about that article. No doubt he thinks we were behind it. But I promise you, we had nothing to do with it."

"He sounded sincere enough when I asked him if he'd seen Jelly," Tess observed. "I honestly don't think he knows anything about her disappearance."

"It does seem an odd coincidence that the whole thing happened right in front of him, though." LuAnn shrugged. "You would think he'd have noticed something."

"To be fair, he was busy grooming a dog at the time," Andy said.

"True." LuAnn chewed her lip.

Tess shrugged. "I can see how Russ might have missed it. You know how it is when you get busy. The whole place could burn down around you, and you'd never see it because you're so hyper-focused."

"That's how Winnie is when she's baking."

"Exactly." Tess stifled a yawn. "I'm ready to get out of here. I want to go back to the inn and put my feet up. It's been a great day, but my feet are starting to ache from being on them so much."

"You'll have to tell me how it went at the Paws on Wheels event."

"I will." The most wonderful feeling came over her as she thought about how she'd spent her morning. "There's a lot to tell."

They said their goodbyes to Andy then walked out of the arena, away from the crowd. As soon as they stepped outside, LuAnn gasped.

"Tess, look!"

Tess looked around, through the crowd forming at the ticket window. "What am I looking at?"

"That dog over there...that cocker spaniel." LuAnn nudged her with her elbow. "That looks just like Jelly!"

"Are you sure?"

"Same coloring. Same cut. Same docked tail. I'm telling you, that dog is Angelica!"

They raced over to the woman, but Tess stopped short. She glanced LuAnn's way and sighed. "We can't just approach a total stranger and ask if her dog is stolen."

"Follow my lead," LuAnn said. She approached the woman and knelt down to scratch the dog behind the ears. "What a beautiful dog you have."

"Oh, thank you!" The woman's cheeks flushed pink. "We're so proud of him. Matthew Crawley is the finest spaniel we've ever owned."

"Matthew Crawley?" LuAnn repeated.

"Yes, we named him after the character from *Downton Abbey*. Are you a fan?"

"Of dogs or the TV show?"

"The TV show."

"Oh, sure." Tess leaned down to pet the dog, paying close attention to its features. "So he's a boy, then?"

"Well, yes. Of course." The woman laughed. "Why else would we name him Matthew?"

Tess rose and did her best not to glare at LuAnn. "He's a *boy* dog, LuAnn. What do you think about that?"

"I, well…" LuAnn patted him on the head. "I think he's the finest black-and-white male cocker spaniel I've ever seen, and I wish him the best in his event."

"We're not here for the regular competition," his owner explained. "Matthew Crawley is going to be competing in an agility round in less than an hour. You should see this boy run! He's got the best time in his age group. Why don't you stick around and watch him in action?"

"I wish we could," Tess said. "But we have to get back to work."

They did, after all.

She and LuAnn chatted as they made their way toward the car, which was parked next to the Paws on Wheels bus.

"So, it went well this morning?" LuAnn asked.

"It was great. I'll tell you all about it on the way home." Tess walked to the passenger side of the car and waited until she heard the familiar *click* as LuAnn unlocked the door. Just as she reached for the handle, she heard barking coming from inside the bus. Her gaze shifted in that direction. There wasn't a person in sight, but the barking continued, louder than before. The dog sounded almost frantic. No doubt the absence of the other dogs had put the poor thing into a panic. Hopefully Jordan and the others would do their best to calm the situation.

"It's kind of sad that one poor dog has to wait for its new owner," LuAnn said as she opened the driver's side door.

"Yeah, I agree. Poor thing is all alone on the bus now."

Still, as she climbed into the car, something about the barking dog raised alarm bells. Tess had that strange feeling in the pit of her stomach that something about the situation wasn't right.

# Chapter Twelve

Tess and LuAnn chatted all the way back to the inn. Tess shared all the morning's events, and with much enthusiasm.

LuAnn eased the car into a lane of heavy traffic as they neared the center of town. "You've sure changed your tune, Tess. You haven't been as enthused about dogs as some of the rest of us, but this morning's event seems to have transformed you."

"I got to see firsthand how these adoptions change lives for the better. I could see the parallels, and it really hit me that God brings dogs and people together."

"I might have to lend my financial support to the organization. Sounds like they're doing a fine work."

"They are." Tess went on to explain how LuAnn could become a Golden Paws sponsor, and before long her friend was laughing all over again. "I just can't believe this conversation we're having, Tess. It's like you're a completely different person."

They arrived back at the inn to discover that they had an unexpected visitor. Winston James. Again.

As soon as she and LuAnn entered the front door, he rose from the sofa and walked their way, beaming as if they were old friends. He greeted them with a rousing, "There you are!" And then extended his hands, as if welcoming guests to his own home.

"Winston." Tess slid her purse strap off her shoulder and set the purse behind the registration desk. "I didn't realize you were coming back to the inn."

"Well, I had a few more questions for you, but you disappeared so quickly after the event this morning. I knew you'd eventually turn up here, so I took a chance."

"I see. Well, we went to lunch. Everyone was hungry. After lunch I went back to the arena to watch some of the agility rounds," she added, "but got distracted looking for Jelly."

Worry lines appeared on his forehead. "Still no word on that missing dog?"

"No, and I don't know what to think anymore. We can only pray that if she wandered out of the building, some kind person took her in and is caring for her."

"Surely that's the case." The lines on his forehead smoothed. "She's such a sweet little thing. A little on the feisty, yappy side, but sweet. Such a shame that there's a dark cloud hanging over this competition, especially in light of the problems the organization has had this year."

"Problems?"

"Well, sure. Don't you read the *Canine Companion*?"

"No, I confess I don't." She fought the temptation to kick off her shoes. What she really wanted was a tall glass of iced tea and the sofa, not a lengthy conversation with a man who made the hair on her arms stand up.

"So you haven't seen any of my articles?" He looked genuinely disappointed.

"I'm afraid not."

The lines between his eyes deepened. "I see. Well, I just assumed you knew about the problems with the competition. The president just resigned a few weeks ago. There was some scandal about misappropriation of funds. I broke the story in the *Companion* a while back. And now a dog goes missing at their biggest annual event? This whole organization is going south in a hurry." He put his hands up, as if admitting defeat. "But, who am I? Just a writer. I've been saying for years that there was corruption and greed at these competitions, but no one would listen to me. Maybe now they will, when they see how low people will go to get what they want. That missing dog is the icing on the cake."

"Icing on the cake?" LuAnn repeated his words, as if not quite believing he would phrase it that way.

"You know what I mean. It's the proof that all I've been saying is true."

Weird, but he almost sounded happy about that. Or maybe he just liked juicy news bits because they increased his chances of selling articles to the magazine.

"Anyway, I'm doing my best to come up with clues that lead to the missing dog, but I keep hitting dead ends. Sounds like everyone else has almost given up."

"We'll never give up, Winston." Andy's voice sounded from behind them. Tess turned to discover the whole family had entered the lobby through the front door. *Ack.* Hopefully they hadn't heard much.

"We love her, and we'll keep searching for her until she's found. And trust me when I say it's not the icing on our cake that she has gone missing. It's devastating."

"Hey, I'm not saying you should give up." Winston waved his hands, as if conceding an argument. "That's what we writers do. We put the information out there for people to make their own judgments. I'm all for keeping the story front and center where it belongs."

Tandi's jaw clenched. "She's more than just a story."

"Right, right."

Andy pushed the button for the elevator, and the family disappeared into it a couple of awkward minutes later. Tess could tell from their sour expressions that Winston had struck a nerve, and not in a good way.

"Wow, he's in a mood," Winston said. "You would think he'd lost a family member, not a dog."

"To them, Jelly is a family member." Tess gazed at him, more perplexed than anything. "But you know what that feels like, right? Didn't you tell me that your dog was your best friend before your wife took him away from you? I would think you'd empathize with the Lawsons, since you've been through something similar in your own life."

"Oh, I do, I do. And sure, I'm good friends with my dog." He waved his hand, as if to dismiss any concerns Tess might have on that matter. "Maybe Andy's just tired. Regardless, I don't think I'm going to get any more information out of him today."

"You're right," Tess said.

"Yes, agreed." LuAnn excused herself to go into the office to work.

Tess needed to take care of some things related to the running of the inn as well, but she didn't know how to shake

Winston. He seemed determined to make himself a permanent fixture.

"I actually came here hoping for lunch," he explained, "but the café was just about to close when I arrived. Even though I was the only customer, that nice lady Winnie let me order some of her delicious soup." He rubbed his belly. "She's a prize. Quite the cook, I'd say."

"Yes, she's top notch."

As if she'd been summoned to enter at just that moment, Winnie emerged from the kitchen, her apron covered in flour.

"What are you working on in there?" Tess asked in the hopes of redirecting the conversation away from the Lawsons and onto something else.

"Pies. I've finished the first four. I've got two more to bake, and then I'm out of here for the night."

"Pies? Yum." Winston's eyes widened. "I thought I smelled something sweet."

"Winnie's known for her baking."

"My stomach is known for liking baked goods." He laughed. "I guess this means I have to come back for lunch tomorrow."

Tess bit her tongue to avoid letting a sarcastic "Yippee!" slip out. She turned her attention to Winnie, who looked absolutely exhausted. The poor woman looked as if she might topple over at any moment.

"You should go home, Winnie. Get some rest."

"I will, as soon as these last two pies are done."

"I'll be happy to watch them for you. Please go home and get some sleep."

"I just hope that stupid dog doesn't keep me up all night again. I'm ready to go over to that place and give that renter a piece of my mind." She mumbled to herself as she left the room.

"Man, I know what she means. Yapping dogs are not my cup of tea either." Winston rolled his eyes. "If I never hear another one after this week I'll be just fine. Horace loves to bark. I need to invest in earplugs."

"I thought your wife was keeping him."

"Ex-wife." He paused. "Hey, are you guys going to keep the inn open to dogs after this week?"

Tess shrugged. "If you'd asked me that a few days ago I would've given you a flat no. But after this morning, seeing how precious those dogs were, I'm more open to the idea. I guess it's true what they say—dogs really are man's best friend."

"Some dogs...and some men." He laughed.

The front door opened, and Reena sashayed in with Beauvine in her arms. Richard came directly behind her with Schmaltzy on a leash. The two were absolutely giddy.

"Well, hello." Tess offered a warm smile. "Long time, no see. How did it go in the booth?"

"Wonderful. We had nearly forty people sign up to give monthly donations." Reena beamed with delight as she shared this news.

"This influx of donations is all thanks to this precious woman." Richard rested his hand on Reena's shoulder. "She's a wonder."

"Oh, hush now. I'm no such thing." Reena's cheeks flushed pink.

"What's going on at the competition tomorrow?" Tess asked. "Will you be going back?"

"More of the agility rounds," Richard explained. "And, of course, the groomers have a competition of their own."

"What? Really?" This surprised Tess.

Winston interrupted the conversation to explain. "Yes, they have races to see who can groom the fastest and the cleanest, that sort of thing. Things get a little crazy. It's a lot of fun to watch." He paused and then looked around the room. "Is there a restroom nearby?"

Tess pointed toward the small guest bath, and he took off in that direction.

As soon as the door clicked, Richard looked Tess's way, worry lines deepening on his forehead. "There's something about that man that hits me the wrong way. I can't put my finger on it, but I don't trust him. Just a feeling, I guess."

"I got the feeling Jordan feels the same way, but they have a history, so it's understandable."

Reena shrugged. "He seems nice. And he interviewed all those people today. I'm hoping he'll write a lovely article to help promote Paws on Wheels. Wouldn't it be something if our story ended up in the *Canine Companion*?"

"Sure would." Richard smiled at her. "Reena, the work you're doing with Jordan and his wife is admirable. I'm so proud of you."

"Really?"

"Well, sure. A lot of folks in our age group would be playing canasta or watching old movies on TV."

"I like to do those things too." She gave him a wink.

"Me too. But the point is, you're still giving of yourself to others. That's a mighty fine thing in my book."

"Thank you, Richard. I appreciate those kind words."

Tess felt like an intruder in their conversation, so she decided to chime in. "Did you guys hear Jordan say that some people do DNA tests on their dogs? That's mind boggling to me. It seems like a lot of effort to go to for a dog."

"Some people really care about things like that," Richard said.

"I have no problem with DNA tests," Tess explained. "In fact, I'm waiting on my results right now. They should be in any day. It just seems strange that some folks would do the same thing for a family pet."

"It's more common than you think," Richard explained. "I did Schmaltzy's, just to make sure he's the real deal."

"I should do Beauvine's to find out if he's more Chihuahua or wiener dog." Reena shrugged. "Not that I would love him any more or less if he's none of the above. He's my little doll baby." She grew silent, and a faraway look came over her. When she finally spoke, her words were softer, more introspective. "It's so funny. My family was all about pedigree. Our people came from old money, and the bloodlines were all people cared about." She turned to face Tess. "When you get your results, let me know. I've been working on genealogy projects for years. It's kind of my thing. I'll be happy to help you go over your results. Unless you think I'm prying, of course."

"I'd be happy to have your input, Reena. I certainly don't know anything about the process, at least not yet."

"It's my cup of tea."

LuAnn entered the room, loaded down with a stack of mail. "What's your cup of tea?"

"Did someone say tea?" Winston entered the room from the bathroom. "Is it tea time? I'd love to sit down for a few minutes and talk with you guys about the competition. I need more material for my article."

"Winston, if you're looking for a story, you don't have to go any further than right here." Tess pointed at LuAnn. "A few days back she told me the most remarkable tale about a dog that had ties to our inn."

"Is that right?"

LuAnn nodded and set the mail down on the registration desk. "Yep. See, there was this mastiff named Jack who served as a mascot for the Confederate troops. He switched sides and ended up with the Union 103rd Division."

"The dog had a change of heart?" Winston asked.

"No. He just ended up in the hands of the North, is all. And, from what I could gather, they treated him well, so he attached himself to them."

"Oh, yes," Reena said. "Dogs have a way of attaching themselves to us, all right."

"And vice versa. Anyway, my point is, he ended up befriending a young Union soldier named Alexander, and they were best buds. Nothing could separate them, at least not for several months. Then, sadly, Alexander was killed in battle."

"This is a tragic story." Winston reached for his notepad. "But very intriguing. Do you mind if I write this down?"

"Of course not. I told you it was newsworthy."

"Did the division keep him on?"

"No, that's the best part of the story. The men in the 103rd cared more about their lost friend than themselves. They decided to transport Jack to Philadelphia, to Alexander's home, thinking he would bring comfort to the family."

"Nice. Always like to add a personal angle to a story." Winston scribbled a few lines onto his page.

"Along the way, the soldier responsible for Jack's transport was injured in a skirmish. A family of slaves traveling toward the Riverfront House found him and tended to his wounds. They managed to get him to Prudence and Jason's place."

"This just gets better and better." Winston looked up from his notepad. "Where was this Riverfront House?"

"You're sitting in it. Wayfarers was once known as the Riverfront House."

"Wow." He jotted down the notes. "Jack was really right here, in this very building?"

"Yes, and the wounded soldier was cared for in a nearby home, owned by a woman named Prudence. She's the one who kept the diary, which is how I discovered all of this."

"Wow, I'd love to see that diary."

LuAnn rose and took a couple of steps toward the office. "I'll be back in a minute," she called back over her shoulder. She left and then returned shortly with her copy of Prudence's diary tucked under her arm.

"So, that's an actual Civil War era diary?" Winston reached, as if expecting LuAnn to hand it to him.

She kept a tight grip on it but responded, "It is, indeed." She took a seat and opened it to the page in question. "Here we go. This is from an entry dated April 3, 1862." Tess began to read aloud.

The monstrous dog came to a stop in front of me, drops of water falling off of his long tongue as he panted heavily. His big brown eyes stared into mine with such force, they caused me to freeze in place. Was he trying to convey a message? I wanted to run, but was afraid he would follow me. With a dog this size chasing me, I wouldn't stand a chance. Off in the distance, an unfamiliar man appeared. I guessed him to be a slave. He called off the dog, who relaxed at once, then rolled over and offered his belly for a rub.

"So, that's the day she met Jack?" Winston asked.

"Yes."

"And the man with him?"

"Really was a slave. He was traveling north with his family."

"I see." Winston raked his fingers through his hair. "But what about the soldier?"

"Prudence's account of meeting him is written that same day." Tess cleared her throat and continued to read.

The two were traveling with four packages—two were small ones—and a badly wounded Union soldier.

I felt the wind go out of me as I saw what bad shape the soldier was in. How would I tend to this man and still get the family safely into the inn? My thoughts were as scrambled as the eggs I'd cooked for Moses's breakfast.

When I finally calmed myself, I did the only thing that made sense—I sent the packages on ahead and went to fetch Jason so he could help me carry the soldier to our home.

"So she and this Jason fellow took the soldier in?" Winston looked up from his notebook. "They sound like good people."

"Very good people," Tess chimed in.

"And she cared for the soldier until he recovered?" Winston asked.

"Well, that's the tricky part," LuAnn responded. "The man was in far worse shape than she thought."

"He didn't make it?" Winston asked.

"I believe I'll let you discover that for yourself." LuAnn closed the diary. "If you research online you will find the story told in great detail."

"Along with Prudence's diary entries?" Winston asked.

"No. Her diary isn't found online."

"Okay. I get it. I'll do the legwork for the story on my own." He closed his notebook and shoved the pen into the spirals. "So, is that why you ladies opened up the inn to dogs, because of your ties to that famous canine?"

LuAnn shrugged. "No. I just love dogs. They're faithful, loyal companions."

"Sounds like Jack really loved his master," Richard said.

LuAnn nodded. "Oh yes. He loved all of those men. And they could have kept him there, in service after Alexander died. But they knew the dog would bring comfort to Alexander's family."

"Wow, there's a lot of sacrifice in this story, isn't there?" Winston noted.

"For sure. But when it comes to dogs, there's often sacrifice involved. People sacrifice their time to train and love the dogs, then the dogs sacrifice their very lives for the owners they love."

Winston set his notebook on the table. "Well, when you put it like that."

Tess glanced over at Huck, who lay curled up at the edge of the sofa. "He's pretty loyal."

"Most dogs are." LuAnn leaned down and scratched Huck behind the ear. "God knew what He was doing when He created them."

Tess nodded, and a lump rose to her throat. "I'm learning to look at him in a new light, with more appreciation. And I love the parallel—Paws on Wheels is taking precious pups from the South and rescuing them, leading them to the North, to new homes, new possibilities."

"Ah, I see. I hadn't thought about it that way before. Now there's a fine angle." Winston turned his attention back to the notepad.

She wanted to say, "Not everything is an angle" but didn't.

Winston turned to face Reena and Richard. "That Jordan Sellers seems like a nice kid, doesn't he? And the wife is pretty nice too. It's a great thing they're doing together, saving all of those dogs. Very...admirable."

"Very." Reena's eyes filled with tears. "I'm so impressed by him."

"I wasn't so sure at first," Richard chimed in. "First time he saw me with my purebred, he lit into me, like I'd done something wrong. But he's growing on me, especially now that I see why he's so passionate about adoption."

Reena nodded. "He is pretty adamant that everyone should feel the way he does about choosing adoption over shopping for a purebred, but he's a dog lover, through and through."

"But there are some great purebred dogs out there," Richard countered. "And there are some decent breeders too. I love purebred dogs."

"True." Winston shrugged. "But I'm still glad he's working so hard to save the no-name brands."

Tess wanted to continue the conversation but found herself distracted after the word *breeders* came into the conversation. She was reminded of the puppy mill she and LuAnn had seen. Had the police gone out there? If so, had they removed the animals? Surely if they'd located Jelly, the Lawsons would have been told by now, right?

Winston released a long, exaggerated yawn. "Sorry, folks, but I've got to get back to Horace. I left him alone, and he doesn't do well without me."

"Your wife—er, ex-wife doesn't have him?" Tess asked.

"Not today. She's busy."

"I still haven't met Horace yet," Tess said. "You'll have to bring him up to the arena tomorrow."

"Right. Yes, of course. I'll see if my ex is going to be back up there tomorrow to watch the grooming challenges. She loves those."

"It would be lovely to meet her."

"Easy for you to say." He flashed a crooked grin and then headed out of the room.

As soon as she was sure their unexpected guest was gone, Tess breathed a sigh of relief.

"He sure asks a lot of questions." Reena eased her way down on the sofa, nearly dropping Beauvine in the process. She settled down, and the pooch curled up in her lap.

"Do you think he'll add us to his article?" Richard asked.

"Maybe." Tess wasn't sure how she felt about that, or whether or not she'd like to be included in one of his articles.

Richard sat next to Reena, and before long they were deep in a conversation that didn't include Tess at all. They only had eyes for each other.

A short while later, the front door opened, and Janice brushed inside, arms loaded down with bags from the craft store.

"Wow, someone did some shopping." Reena's eyes bugged as she turned her attention away from Richard and onto Janice. "I thought *I* liked to shop."

"Zelda asked me to help with the centerpieces for the wedding. I said yes." Janice did her best to hold on to the bags, but one of them slipped out of her hand and onto the floor. "Oops."

Tess grabbed it and offered to take a couple more as well.

Reena and Richard went back to chatting, and LuAnn gestured for Tess and Janice to join her in the office. Once there, Janice set her bags down. "Whew! I'm glad to be rid of those."

LuAnn shut the door behind them, which made Tess think she had something private to share with them.

"Is everything okay?" she asked.

"Yes, I've just been in here doing a little research." LuAnn took a seat behind the desk and turned her attention to the computer.

"Research?" Tess asked.

"Yes." LuAnn gestured for Tess to take a seat in front of the computer. Tess did so and then stared at the screen. "What am I looking at?"

"I pulled up the online version of the *Canine Companion*. See that search box right there?" LuAnn pointed to the screen. "Type in his name."

"Is this one of those deals where you have to have a subscription to read it online?" Janice asked.

Tess shook her head as she examined the site in front of her. "No. They have older issues online, anyway. I don't see March or April, at least not yet."

A search for the name Winston James brought up several articles inside the *Canine Companion* publication. In fact, the most recent one she could locate was the infamous article about Russ Schumer and Jelly. She glanced over that article, then skimmed several others. After a few minutes, she signed out of the *Canine Companion* site.

"What are you doing?" LuAnn asked. "We were just getting started."

"I want to do a more general search on the internet, outside of that publication." Tess typed in *Winston James freelance writer* and several more articles came up. After a moment she stumbled across one with yet another familiar name.

"Oh, wow, look at this." Tess pointed to the screen. "Here's an interview Winston did with Jordan Sellers for the *Houston Chronicle*. It's also dated two years ago."

"What does it say?"

"Well, it's about his organization." She skimmed the article. "And there's some backstory here, about why Jordan got into rescuing. Oh my. It looks like he used to be homeless."

"Wow, that's sad."

"Very." She kept skimming. "It's obvious Jordan isn't keen on breeders. It looks like Winston made a pretty big deal out of that fact. He seems to be sensationalizing the negative. And I can't believe Winston would go that far, to reveal so much of Jordan's personal story. Seems pretty intrusive." No wonder Jordan didn't trust Winston James. He'd definitely crossed a line to get a dramatic story.

"Anything else?" LuAnn asked.

Tess continued to read the article. "Oh my. Looks like he's been arrested in the past."

"For what?" LuAnn and Janice spoke in unison.

"I'm not sure. This article doesn't say, but it's obvious Winston is questioning Jordan's integrity after he landed himself in the Harris County Jail."

"What else can you find when you research Jordan's name?" LuAnn asked. "Outside of that one interview with Winston, I mean."

Tess did a quick search and found many, many references to Jordan, all of them positive. "He's quite the hero in the Houston area. Look at this." She pointed at an article about his work after Hurricane Harvey. "And he's even traveled to other southern states with his bus to pick up dogs to bring north."

"Why north?" Janice asked. "I still haven't figured that part out."

"I guess the shelters up north aren't as full?"

Janice rested her hand on her stomach as it growled. "I wonder why that is."

"Me too. Interesting. I'll have to look into it." Tess continued to search until she found a few more articles about Paws on Wheels. "Not everyone is so happy about the transports. Check this out." Tess read aloud. "'The mayor of Houston has been under scrutiny again this week. Instead of focusing on problems at the local animal shelters, she has linked arms with Paws on Wheels to send animals to northern states to adopting homes.'"

"I wonder why that's an issue," LuAnn said. "They're doing a good thing, right?"

Tess skimmed the rest of the article. "I guess some people think they're just putting a Band-Aid on the problem in Texas. But I think it's awesome that they come all this way with those dogs."

Janice disappeared from the room and returned a couple of minutes later with a muffin in hand. "Sorry. I was starving. I've been so busy that I keep forgetting to eat."

"That's not good."

"Let's go back to Winston James." Janice took a bite of her muffin and spoke with a full mouth. "I'm curious to know if any of his *Canine Companion* articles are recent."

Tess did a quick general search. "Nothing for the past couple years. Do you find that odd?"

"Very." Janice took another bite of her muffin and leaned against the wall.

"He's a freelancer, so it's possible he writes for a variety of publications. I think that's how that works. But why would he imply that he still writes for *Canine Companion* if he really doesn't?"

"Maybe he's trying to impress people," LuAnn suggested.

"Maybe," Tess said. She leaned back in the chair, more confused than ever.

# CHAPTER THIRTEEN

The following morning Tess awoke in a fog. She vaguely recalled a moment in the middle of the night where the ding of the elevator bell woke her up. Or had she just dreamed that? Before she could settle the issue in her mind, her cell phone rang. She answered, still half asleep.

"Hi, Tess, it's Randy. I wanted to let you know that we've been working to shut down that puppy mill, thanks to your call."

"Oh, that's wonderful." She stifled a yawn and sat up in the bed.

"Yes, we got another tip that same day, this one from a buyer. It's every bit as bad as you said. Those pictures, as clear as they were, didn't really do the place justice."

"No kidding. So what comes next?"

"We spent yesterday putting together a team. We can't just go in and get the dogs without having a plan. We needed to gather crates, food, a couple of vets, even some vet techs— everything has to be set up and ready to go when we go in. But I wanted you to know that the owner is in custody, and the dogs are now the property of the county. They're in terrible condition, but we've put together a team to rehab them and, hopefully, get them to the point where they are adoptable." He paused and then released a sigh. "By the way, we kept our eyes open for that missing cocker spaniel, but there was no sign of her. This mill specializes in other breeds, primarily dachshunds and Chihuahuas."

"That's a shame." Tess paused to think it through. "But on the other hand, I would hate to think that Angelica would have ended up at a place like that."

"Yes, but we haven't given up the search. We're following a couple of leads right now, in fact."

"Any you can share with me?" she asked.

He cleared his throat.

"Okay, okay." Tess laughed. "You can't blame a girl for trying."

"No, I can't, especially when she's doing her best to help."

"I'm assuming you've checked the local shelters and dog rescue groups?"

"Yes, we're doing all we can. We realize the urgency of this situation. We know she's scheduled to compete tomorrow morning at eleven o'clock at the arena. She's up for Best in Show."

"Right. Well, thank you for working so hard," Tess said. "I know the family appreciates it. They're staying at the inn, which is why I feel so strongly about helping."

"I understand."

"Speaking of Angelica, I meant to ask if you guys got any footage from the cameras at the arena."

"A little," Randy said. "There were so many people jammed into that area it was hard to see through them to where the crate was located on the floor, though. There were people all around it most of the time."

"Any familiar faces in that crowd?"

"Sure. We made a list of several—everyone from a reporter to several of the other competitors. Oh, and that Paws on Wheels guy. He was just passing through on his way to the bus, I think. We're not sure."

"What about the groomer?"

"The big-name one? Russ Schumer?"

"Yes."

"He was at his station in the grooming area, right next to the family lounge. Nothing suspicious. We watched several hours of footage, and he never left his station except to go tend to a dog in a crate nearby." He paused. "Anyway, back to the reason I called. We're going back to the mill late this afternoon to gather the dogs. We've set up a temporary shelter inside the loading dock on the backside of the arena. The local shelter isn't big enough to handle the problems we'll face."

"Where will the dogs go from there?"

"We're not sure yet. This is the biggest case we've handled in Washington County, and it's pretty overwhelming, to be honest. But we'll figure it out."

"I'm sure you will," said Tess.

Randy hesitated. "Anyway, I should let you go. There's a lot to do."

"Thanks again for your help." Tess ended the call, got dressed, and then walked down the stairs and into the kitchen, where she found Janice and LuAnn working on breakfast. The smell of bacon filled the air, as did the luscious aroma of freshly brewed coffee. She looked around the kitchen, a little confused. "Where's Winnie?"

LuAnn looked up from the skillet and brushed a strand of loose hair out of her face with the back of her hand. "She called in. Said she's too exhausted to get out of bed. Something about a dog keeping her up all night."

"Man, it must really be bad, for her to stay in bed," Tess said. "That's not like her at all."

"Tell me about it. I told her not to worry, that we would take care of everything. It's going to mean a lot more work for us, though."

"I'm up for it." Tess paused. "Hey, speaking of middle-of-the-night adventures, did you hear the elevator in the middle of the night? Seems like a nightly occurrence."

"I heard it too," Janice chimed in. "Not sure who it was, though."

"I'm pretty sure it's Richard," LuAnn said. "I got out of bed to check and thought I heard him talking to his dog inside the elevator."

"That makes sense. I guess we're lucky that Huck sleeps through the night without needing to go out."

Janice carried on about breakfast, oblivious to Tess's internal ponderings. "I made pancakes, and LuAnn is almost done with the bacon. We've got all of those muffins Winnie made yesterday, and I pulled a couple of those breakfast casseroles out of the freezer and popped them into the oven. If you count the bowls of fresh fruit in the refrigerator, I think we have enough food on hand to satisfy the breakfast menu."

"Wow, you've really been working. I'm so sorry it took me a while to get downstairs, but I had a call from Randy Lewis. He said they're in the process of collecting all those dogs from the puppy mill. Apparently it's going to be quite the task to get them rehabbed and into new homes. I can't even imagine."

"Oh, I'm so glad to hear those sweet pups are going to get a second chance." LuAnn flipped a slice of bacon over. "What a relief."

"Yes, I'm relieved as well, though it sounds like an overwhelming task, one our fair city wasn't prepared to handle." Tess washed her hands and reached for an apron. "Now, what can I do?"

"You're not planning to go up to the arena again today to watch the agility rounds?" Janice asked.

"No. I'm yours all day. Just tell me what I can do to help."

A look of sheer relief came over her friend's face. "Perfect. Right now you can make sure we're good on dishes, silverware, and napkins for breakfast. Then, you can help us tend to the café guests. After that we'll do dishes and regroup."

"Do you think everyone is coming down for breakfast?" LuAnn asked.

"Reena and Richard were up pretty late talking," Janice responded. "I came down around eleven and saw them still sitting on the sofa."

"Oh?"

"Yes." Janice laughed. "I'm pretty sure they were holding hands, but they separated when I walked in. It was like the parting of the Red Sea."

Tess laughed. "How cute is that?"

"Very." Janice grinned. "But they got to bed late, so they're likely sleeping in. Oh, and Geneva took off early this morning, so I don't expect her for breakfast. I don't have any idea where she went, but she left in a hurry."

"What about the Lawsons?" Tess asked.

"I would imagine they'll be down for breakfast soon." LuAnn turned off the fire under the skillet and transferred the last of the bacon to a paper towel. "They were exhausted last night."

Tess walked out into the café to set the tables. She checked on the coffee, then prepped the plates and napkins. She was just reaching for the silverware when Tandi entered the room with her children. Tess offered a rousing "Good morning," then completed her task by fetching the silverware.

"Good morning to you too." Tandi offered a weak smile.

"Janice will be out in a minute with the pancakes, bacon, and fruit. I hope you're hungry."

"Starving!" Wyatt said. "I love pancakes."

"Me too," Callie echoed.

Andy entered the café and joined Tess at the coffee urn. "We're trying to make this day as normal as possible, for the sake of the kids. They love to watch the agility rounds, so we're headed back up to the arena to be spectators."

Tandi joined them and reached for an empty coffee mug. "I'm trying not to think about tomorrow."

Janice entered the room with the food in hand. "Tomorrow? What's tomorrow?"

"Best in Show," Tess reminded her.

"Jelly was supposed to compete." Tandi filled her mug with coffee. "Only now, of course…" Her words drifted off. "You know."

"Oh, that's right." Janice set the platter of food down. "I understand."

The Lawsons ate their breakfast and then left for the arena. Richard and Reena were no-shows until around nine thirty when they appeared in the café, dressed and ready for their day.

"I just made a fresh pot of coffee," Tess said. "Have a seat, and I'll fill your cups."

Reena nodded and then yawned as she settled down at a nearby table. "Thank you. You read my mind. I'm so tired, I've decided to stay put this morning."

"I might do the same." Richard smiled. "Though I was thinking it might be nice to take Schmaltzy for a leisurely walk along the river after breakfast. Would you and Beauvine like to join us, Reena, or does that sound too taxing?"

"That sounds lovely, if I can wake Beauvine up. He slept like a rock."

"I wish I could say the same." Richard sighed. "Schmaltzy has been up and down all night. Would you believe me if I told you that he made me get out of bed at four in the morning to take him outside? Two nights in a row, in fact."

Well, that explained that.

"I couldn't go back to sleep," Richard explained. "So I did a little browsing on the *Canine Companion* site. I've been looking for that article about the dog who called 911. You'll get such a kick out of it."

"Did you find it?" Tess asked.

He shook his head. "Not yet. I ended up dozing off. But I won't stop looking."

They enjoyed a quick breakfast and then headed upstairs to fetch the dogs for their walk. Tess began to work double time to clear the morning dishes from the café tables and get them washed. With Winnie missing from the kitchen this morning, there was much to be done.

Thorn, their friend and the inn's handyman, showed up around ten thirty to fix a leaky faucet in the downstairs bathroom. Then he tended to another small leak under the kitchen sink. Winnie came buzzing in at ten forty-five, filled with apologies for sleeping in.

"No, I told you to rest," Tess admonished her. "We could have handled this, Winnie."

"I'm fit as a fiddle, now that I've slept a bit," Winnie countered.

Tess prepped the café for their lunch crowd then worked alongside Winnie, Janice, and LuAnn to pull lunch together for their café guests—chicken salad, egg salad, and tomato basil soup. By the time their first lunch guests arrived, Tess was pooped. Still, she had to keep going. LuAnn and Janice managed the kitchen while Tess, Robin, and Taylor served their guests in the café.

Many of the locals showed up, including Paul Townsend and Charlotte Bickerton, who were so infatuated with each other that they hardly noticed the food. Tess was also thrilled when Brad's aunts entered the inn, arm in arm. Thelma and Irene settled in at their favorite table by the window and ordered the chicken salad on croissants. Tess wasn't as happy to see Winston James but offered him a seat near Paul and Charlotte.

Just about the time the café was at its capacity, the front door of the inn opened, and Geneva rushed inside with Gigi in her arms. She raced toward the stairs without saying a word. Tess could tell at a glance that Geneva was crying.

Tess hurried in the young woman's direction and called out to her. "Geneva, are you okay?"

Geneva nodded and held tight to the pup as she ran up the stairs.

Winston joined Tess in the parlor, his gaze on Geneva, who disappeared from sight. "People come and go so quickly around here." He chuckled. "Get it? That's a line from *The Wizard of Oz*." He lifted his hands and, with the voice of the wicked witch, said, "'I'll get you, my pretty, and your little dog too!'" A howl of laughter followed. This garnered the attention of many in the café, who stared at him in surprise.

Tess didn't join in. She was far too worried about Geneva to play along with Winston's attempt at humor.

He leaned in a little too close to whisper, "Maybe there's a story behind those tears. I think I'll go see." He took a step toward the stairs, but Tess grabbed his arm.

"I'm sorry, but I can't let you go to Geneva's room without her permission, Winston. But while I have you here, I do have a question."

"What's that?" He plopped down onto the sofa and put his feet up on the coffee table.

"I looked up some of your articles online."

"Oh?" His face lit up, and she could see the pride in his eyes. "Thanks for telling me. Did you see the big piece I did about the DC dog show? It was in the *Companion* a few months back."

"That doesn't sound familiar."

"Oh, I can't wait for you to read it. The funniest thing happened in the winner's circle." He dove into a story about a Pomeranian who tried to eat the judge's shoes, but Tess only heard half of it. No such article existed on the web, not under his name, anyway. Unless she had overlooked something, Winston hadn't written for the *Canine Companion* for at least two years, since that story he ran on Jelly and Russ Schumer.

"I stumbled across the interview you did with Jordan in the Houston Chronicle a while back."

"Yes. I interviewed him just after Hurricane Harvey. He does great work with those rescues. I seem to recall there's a backstory there. Something about how he went through a season of homelessness himself."

"Yes, I saw that. I was rather startled to see how much of his personal story appeared in the article."

Winston shrugged. "I also seem to remember that he has a...well, a history. We'll just leave it at that."

"Do you mean his arrest?"

Winston stared at her, bug-eyed. "Well, now that you bring it up." He leaned in close, lowering his voice. "Though, between you and me, the guy was arrested for picketing a puppy store. Apparently, he refused to leave when the officer asked him to, so they took him in." Winston chuckled. "He's not exactly Leavenworth material, but I recall having a little fun with that information in my article, if you know what I mean."

"I know exactly what you mean." She bit her lip to keep from saying more.

He paused. "Hey, I might hang out in the café for a bit and drink another cup of coffee. That okay?"

"Sure." Tess walked into the café and reached for a clean cup, which she passed to him as he took a seat at the table he had occupied before.

Janice tapped her on the shoulder and gestured for Tess to join her in the hallway. She pointed at Winston and groaned. "Really? He's back?"

"Yeah, and I don't mind admitting, that guy is getting on my last nerve."

"Mine too, but he's right about one thing—something's wrong with Geneva. I feel like I need to head upstairs to make sure she's okay. She looked so upset."

"I don't know, Janice. It's none of our business."

"If Stacy was in a strange place, completely alone, in tears, I'd want someone to step in and offer her a shoulder to cry on."

"True." Tess lowered her voice. "But what if she's in cahoots with that puppy mill owner? You know? What if she's upset because the police raided the place today, and she was somehow involved in it?"

"You're letting your imagination run away with you, Tess. If she was responsible for that mess, she'd be in jail right now, not sitting in Sunshine and Daisies."

"I guess you're right. I'm not thinking very clearly right now. I'm not sure I will be until Jelly is returned to her rightful owners."

She went back to work, caring for their guests in the café. Winston pulled out his phone and appeared to be browsing the internet while taking sips of his coffee. She left him there, grateful for the fact that he was no longer peppering anyone with questions.

After the café cleared and the inn was quiet, the ladies worked side by side in the kitchen on the dishes.

Winnie slung her dishcloth over her shoulder. "Should I make some oatmeal cookies?"

"For the guests or for us?" Janice asked.

"Both!" Winnie chuckled.

They all ended up making the cookies together. Tess had such a wonderful time laughing and talking with her friends that she almost forgot about the writer who was still seated in the café. Sometime around three thirty she carried a tray of cookies out to the buffet table.

Winston looked up from his spot at the table and shoved his phone into his pocket. "Mmm. Something smells mighty good."

Though he wasn't a guest at the inn, she decided to offer him a cookie anyway. Maybe it would serve as an incentive for him to be on his way. "Help yourself."

He rose and walked toward the buffet, grabbed a cookie, and took a big bite. A delighted look came over his face. "Oh, wow, these are great."

"Thanks." Tess gestured to the kitchen. "Winnie is our star baker."

"Right. I think I read something about that." He took another bite then spoke around the cookie in his mouth. "She won some sort of contest?"

"Yes, and we've got a never-ending supply of flour to prove it."

"Lucky ducks." He took another bite and then sat back down at the café table. Tess wondered if she should tell him that the inn didn't serve dinner. Would he take the hint?

She walked back into the kitchen and fixed a small plate of cookies. "I'm going to take these up to Geneva."

"I thought we were going to leave her alone?" Janice countered.

"Yeah, I know. But dropping off cookies isn't exactly interfering." Tess shrugged. "Anyway, they might cheer her up."

"I want to come too." LuAnn dried her hands on a dishcloth.

"Hold up. I'm tagging along as well." Janice turned off Big Red and brushed her hands on her apron. "You're not finding out what's going on without me."

The three ladies walked out into the parlor, and Winston rose from his seat in the café.

"Going up?" he called out.

"Yes. We'll be back down shortly."

Winston took another bite of his cookie and wiped his hands on his slacks. "Do me a favor?"

"What's that?" Tess asked.

"If you find out anything that might be of interest…" He quirked a brow. "Fill me in when you come back down."

"You want us to share a guest's personal story with you, for an article?" Tess felt her blood begin to boil. "No way."

"Okay, okay." He walked over to the cookie tray and grabbed one before heading for the front door of the inn. "Guess I'll head back up to the arena, then."

"Good riddance," Janice muttered under her breath.

The three ladies climbed the stairs to the third floor. When they got to Geneva's room, Tess reached out to knock on the door. Before she could do so, she heard a conversation going on inside.

Geneva's voice was raised in obvious anguish. "Don't you get it, Victor? I can't keep this up. I'm stuck, and I don't know how to get out of this."

A pause followed, and all three women stood in frozen silence.

"No, I can't tell them," Geneva continued with increasing passion. "I can't. Do you realize what would happen if I did that? Everything Gigi and I have worked for would be over in an instant. I…I…just can't!" Her crying began in earnest now.

"What in the world?" Janice whispered. "Who's Victor?"

Tess shrugged and leaned in closer to hear more.

"I took her out to that place the other day," Geneva continued. "The one I told you about."

"Took who?" LuAnn whispered. "Jelly?"

Tess shrugged. Maybe. Or, maybe not.

"That breeder is horrible. You wouldn't believe me if I told you how awful that place is. It sickened me."

Well, at least they agreed on that.

"But ever since I found out the truth about—" Her words stopped abruptly.

Tess backed away, worried Geneva might have heard them at her door.

"Let's get out of here," Tess whispered.

She and the other ladies headed back down the stairs and eased their way down to the second floor, where they paused.

"What was that about?" Janice asked.

"I have no idea. But apparently she's done something bad." Tess shrugged. "Whatever it is, she's not ready to come clean with it."

"She took someone to that breeder. That's what she said. Do you think she was talking about Angelica or Gigi?"

"I don't know."

The elevator dinged, and the door opened to reveal Reena and Richard in an embrace, lip-locked. They were so lost in the moment that they never saw the ladies.

Unfortunately, the dogs did. Beauvine and Schmaltzy started yapping, but their owners still didn't come up for air.

From inside Geneva's room Tess heard loud wails. She knew she shouldn't eavesdrop, but she was truly concerned for Geneva. She went back upstairs and put her ear against the door of Sunshine and Daisies. Was Geneva in some sort of trouble?

Just about the time she heard the words, "I can't do this anymore!" Tess leaned a bit too hard, the door flew open, and Tess tumbled to the ground, the plateful of cookies flying from one side of the room to the other.

# CHAPTER FOURTEEN

"Ouch!" Tess rubbed her arm and groaned.

Unfortunately, Gigi went into a protective barking fit and headed straight for her. Tess put her hands up to cover her face, in case the dog decided to attack.

"Gigi, no! Oh my goodness, I'm sorry!" Geneva did her best to get the dog under control then turned her attention to Tess. "I had no idea you were out there." She quickly ended her call with the words, "I'm sorry, Victor, but I have to go," and tossed the phone on her bed.

Tess rose and stretched to make sure nothing was broken. She groaned again when she saw the mess on the floor. "I'm so sorry, Geneva. We just finished baking some cookies, and I was bringing some up as a surprise. I never meant to make a goober of myself and a mess of your room, all at the same time."

"It's okay. Really. I was just on the phone with my brother. He's the one I call when I need advice. I'll call him back later."

Tess, Janice, and LuAnn began to pick up the cookies. When they finished, Tess noticed that Geneva had tears in her eyes.

"I'm s-s-sorry!" Geneva's voice quivered as she attempted to speak. "I'm just a mess today. P-please forgive me."

Tess was suddenly filled with compassion for the young woman. So was Gigi, apparently. The little canine took to leaping up and down next to her owner.

"Is there anything we can do to help, honey?" LuAnn asked.

"I—I don't know. I don't think anyone can help. I'm a wreck." She paused and then gestured for the women to enter her room. "Please come in. I need to talk to someone, or I'll just bust."

"Of course." The ladies spoke in unison. Geneva gestured for them to sit on the edge of the bed.

Geneva paced the room, finally coming to a stop in front of them. "I got some news a couple of days ago, and it has devastated me." Her nose crinkled, and for a moment Tess thought she might start crying all over again.

"I can see that," Tess said. "But what happened?"

Tears brimmed on Geneva's lashes. "I bought Gigi a few years ago from a breeder I thought was reputable, a Mrs. Matranga. Everything seemed aboveboard. I chose Gigi from an online site the Matranga family runs. I honestly thought she only had the mother and father dog and a litter of pups. That's what she led me to believe, anyway." Geneva wiped her nose with the back of her hand. "In retrospect, I did find it odd that she didn't ask me to meet her at her house, but sometimes people are weird about stuff like that. You know? I would be."

"Understandable," LuAnn chimed in. "You don't want to give total strangers access to your house."

"Right. Anyway, Mrs. Matranga asked me to meet her in the parking lot at this discount tire place not far from where she lives. When I got there, she had Gigi in her arms. Gigi was such a sweet little thing, and so tiny. I'd been dying to own a purebred shorthaired dachsie because that's what we had when I was growing up. So, I paid for her, got her American Kennel Club paperwork and shot records, and left without ever knowing anything more about the woman who'd sold her to me. Gigi was perfect…only she wasn't."

"She wasn't?" Tess asked.

"No, she had kennel cough, a bad case. I didn't realize it until I got her back home. I took her to the vet, and he started her on antibiotics and cough syrup right away. She recovered, but I was really worried for a while there." Geneva paused and scooped the pup into her arms. "This little girl has been my baby." More tears came. "And I know people think I'm crazy for spoiling her and dressing her up, but if they knew the truth, they would understand why."

"The truth?" Tiny creases formed between Janice's brows as she posed the question.

"Yes." Geneva plopped down on the end of the bed. "The truth is, she's probably the only 'baby' I'll ever have."

"What do you mean?" LuAnn asked.

"When I—I was f-fourteen, I was diagnosed with uterine cancer."

"Oh, honey." LuAnn's eyes widened. "I'm so sorry."

"The doctors performed surgery to save my life. Of course, it was a devastating blow, to be told as a teenager that I could never have babies of my own." Her eyes brimmed with tears, and before long she was crying in earnest.

Tess slipped an arm over Geneva's shoulders and allowed her to cry, long and hard. "Such awful news. I'm so sorry."

"I haven't really dated anyone seriously because, how could I? What if I fall in love with Mr. Right, then have to tell him that I can't ever give him children? What kind of a man is going to stick around after hearing that?"

LuAnn held her tight. "If he's really Mr. Right, he'll be open to the idea of adopting or fostering."

"No. It's easier to just bury that part of my life and forget about it. So, I love on Gigi here. She's my baby."

"Of course." Now Tess understood—everything.

"I've paraded her around like a little dolled-up princess and enjoyed the attention. I'll admit it. But something happened a couple of days ago that has changed our lives." Geneva chewed her lip. "I got some terrible news."

"You can tell us, Geneva." LuAnn patted her on the shoulder. "We'll help if we can."

"It happened just after Gigi won Best in Breed. I happened to overhear someone at the arena mention a local breeder named Matranga, and not in a positive light. That was my first clue that the woman I'd purchased Gigi from ran an actual puppy mill. I kept listening in and learned that the Matrangas—there's a Mr. and Mrs.—sometimes falsify the AKC paperwork on the puppies they sell."

"Wait—falsify the paperwork?" This made no sense to Tess. "How is that possible?"

"Well, it's complicated, but apparently several years ago, many litters back, they forged the paperwork for a male dachshund named Colonel Potter. He was named after the character—"

"On *M.A.S.H*?" LuAnn asked.

"Right. Anyway, from what I overheard the other day, Colonel Potter was born to a female that had no paperwork. The Matrangas managed to forge his papers by saying he'd been born in a different litter altogether. I suppose breeders do that sometimes. They often have multiple litters to care for at once, and I'm sure things get confusing. But this time it was done deliberately, to give the pups a name that was never really theirs."

"I can see how easy it would be for them to do that," LuAnn said. "Wrong, but easy."

"Yes. And from what I overheard, Colonel's Potter's real mama dog was a purebred, but there was no proof of her lineage. So he was the real deal, just no papers to prove it."

"That's a bummer," said Tess.

"Right. But once the Matrangas changed his paperwork to say he was born in a separate litter, the deed was done. He was AKC registered, and no one knew the difference. They went on to breed him and other litters were born. Jump ahead a few years, and Gigi came into the world. Colonel Potter was her great-grandfather."

"So, are you saying that every litter born in Colonel Potter's line wasn't"—how did Geneva say it?—"the real deal?"

"Right." Tears sprang to Geneva's eyes. "My little baby *is* a purebred. Look at her. She's got every marking. She's got the paperwork. But the paperwork isn't valid if this story is true." Geneva erupted in tears again. "That means she's not able to compete. And don't even get me started on how disappointed I am about that. I'm completely devastated."

Tess didn't interrupt as the young woman went into a lengthy explanation of how this would affect poor Gigi's life.

"Don't you see? She loves to compete. It's her life. Only, now she can't."

"Aren't there ways around this?" Janice asked. "I would think this is a common problem, what with so many breeders involved."

"I don't know." Geneva released a slow breath. "But I wanted to find out for myself, so I did some quick research online right after I overheard this story. I found an address for a family named Matranga on the outskirts of town. I did the bravest thing I've ever done. I drove out to their house." She pinched her eyes shut and shook her head. "I was terrified. But I think Mrs. Matranga was more scared than I was, to be honest. She had no clue I was coming or how I located her. And when I started questioning her, she got angry and threatened to call the police."

"She would never have wanted the police to show up at her place," Tess said. "They would have shut her down immediately."

"Right!" Geneva gave her an inquisitive look. "Wait, you've seen it? Do you ladies know the Matrangas?"

"Oh, I..." Tess and LuAnn looked at each other then shifted their gaze back to Geneva. "No, I don't know anyone by that name," Tess said.

"Well, don't bother trying to get to know them. I certainly didn't envision my Gigi coming from such a horrible place." She pulled the dog close and planted kisses on her head.

"You couldn't have known, Geneva," LuAnn said. "The woman is a fraud and a thief. What she's doing is illegal."

"Yes. And now I see why breeders usually meet potential buyers in different locations. I'm sickened by what I saw there. Anyone with a heart would be." She pulled Gigi close. "When I think that my little baby was born in that awful place, it makes my stomach churn."

"I'm glad you got her out," Janice said.

"Horrible." Geneva shook her head. "I just want to give her the best life possible. She's young, with so much potential. I hate that she can't compete anymore, I just hate it."

"Is there a way to prove her lineage through DNA?" Tess asked. "I just heard that they're doing it on dogs now."

"Yes, I could have her tested, but DNA profiles can't determine a dog's breed or if they're purebred. Though…" She paused and appeared to be thinking. "A lot of competitors are doing the test voluntarily to prove that their dogs are from particular bloodlines. There's a program with the AKC for owners and breeders. Basically, it eliminates questions about parentage."

"That sounds intriguing," LuAnn said. "How does it work?"

"Every pup that's tested gets a unique DNA profile number, which is attached to all AKC certificates and pedigrees." Geneva's shoulders slumped. "I honestly don't know what to do. Is it worth putting her—and me—through all of that, or should I just give up on the dream of seeing her ever win Best in Show?"

"That's a tough question, for sure." Tess tried to think of something brilliant to say, but nothing came to her.

"If I didn't have a conscience, I'd just move forward and let Gigi compete on Saturday. No one would ever know the difference." Geneva sighed. "The problem is, I *do* have a conscience."

"I think the whole thing is just awful," LuAnn said. "Horrible. If Gigi's great-grandfather was a purebred, what do a few papers have to do with anything?"

"Unfortunately, they have everything to do with it."

Janice snapped her fingers. "Well, if DNA can prove parentage, then maybe it can prove Colonel Potter's parentage. Is he still alive?"

Geneva nodded. "Yes, I asked about him and was told he's getting up there in years. But this is a complicated and lengthy process, and I can't demand the owner get him tested. The point is, Gigi can't compete on Saturday. I'll have to withdraw her from the competition, and that breaks my heart." Geneva burst into tears all over again.

"I'm sure you're devastated."

Geneva eventually calmed herself enough to speak. "I—I called the p-police, by the way. Yesterday morning."

"You did?" Tess was shocked to hear this. "What did they say?"

"They called back this morning to say they were going to get the dogs out of there this afternoon. I think that's why I'm so emotional. This whole thing has me feeling sick inside, but knowing Gigi's breeder is going to jail only complicates things. What if I have to testify? Ugh."

"Look at it as a blessing. You'll get to help put a stop to her illegal breeding practices for good, so no other animals have to receive that kind of treatment."

This seemed to calm Geneva immensely.

"Yes, you'll be doing all of those dogs a huge favor if you testify." LuAnn patted her arm. "Think of all the little dogs you'll be protecting."

"True." She wiped her eyes with the back of her hand, then gave the ladies a look of gratitude. "Thank you for listening."

"Are you kidding? We're here for you, Geneva. If you need anything else…" Tess wasn't sure how to complete the sentence. "Well, you know where we are."

"I'm grateful for your kindness." Geneva sighed. "And I know Gigi is too. She's really enjoyed her time here."

"Tell you what." Tess rose and took a couple of steps toward the door. She stopped to grab the plate from the dresser top. "I'm going back downstairs to get you a fresh plate of cookies. Do you like oatmeal?"

"They're my favorite."

"Perfect."

The Inn Crowd walked down the stairs together in silence. No doubt they were all absorbing what they'd just heard. When they got to the kitchen, Tess grabbed a clean plate and put four cookies on it. Before carrying it up, she gave LuAnn and Janice a sheepish look. "I didn't have the courage to tell her we followed her to the puppy mill. Should I?"

LuAnn shook her head. "Eventually, but not right now. We don't want to give her more to be upset about."

"True. But when I come back downstairs I want to get online and check out that name, Matranga. Does it sound familiar to either of you?"

"Not at all," Janice said.

"Never heard of them," LuAnn echoed.

Tess found Geneva in a much calmer state when she took the cookies up. Before they parted ways, Tess told her that she would be praying for her. This seemed to lift Geneva's spirits.

"You would do that for me?"

"Well, of course, hon."

A hint of a smile tipped up the corners of her mouth. "My grandma used to do that for me."

"I'm always happy to pray for our guests, and I consider you and Gigi to be among my favorite of all time."

"That means a lot. Thank you, Tess." Geneva chuckled then reached for a cookie. "Hey, one more question."

"What's that?"

"I've heard there's a sweet little dress shop in town. A boutique?"

"Do you mean Antoinette's Closet?"

"Yes, I believe that's it."

"Our friend Emma owns it. She's very cute and trendy, and so is her place. I think you'll love it."

"Does she sell dog-wear?"

"You mean outfits for dogs?" Tess shrugged. "Beats me. But maybe she will start, after this."

"Oh, she should. You'd be surprised to see how many people love to dress like their dogs." She paused and giggled. "I guess I got that backward. You'd be surprised at how many people like to dress up their dogs to match their own attire."

"I'm figuring that out."

"I think I'll get out for a while and go see her shop. Do you think she's still open?"

"For another hour or so, I think."

"Perfect."

Their conversation ended on a happy note, thank goodness. Geneva was all smiles as she headed out to shop. Funny, how something so simple could turn things around.

A few minutes later the ladies all met in the office, and Tess made her way to the computer. As it booted up, they talked about what they'd learned upstairs.

Tess felt her eyes grow moist as she thought about the sobs she'd heard from Geneva. "It just breaks my heart, what she told us about not being able to have children."

"So sad," Janice agreed. "But it also explains why she and Gigi are so close. That dog really is like her child. No wonder she dresses her up and treats her like a baby."

The computer finally booted up. Just as Tess started to open the browser, a notification appeared at the top right-hand side of the screen. Her breath caught in her throat when she saw that it was from the ancestry site. "Oh my goodness, look!" She pointed to the notification.

"Is that what I think it is?" LuAnn pulled up a chair to get a better look.

"Yes, my DNA results are in."

Janice let out a squeal. "This is so exciting!"

"Should I look at the results first, before checking out the Matrangas?"

"Who cares about the Matrangas?" LuAnn laughed. "This is all about you now. Check out your results, Tess. You've been waiting for weeks."

"Okay." She clicked on "DNA Story," but her hand almost slipped off the mouse. "I don't know why my palms are sweating."

She clicked the globe icon, and it started spinning around. It finally halted, and her results came into view. She read the numbers aloud. "'Sixty-one percent England, Wales, and Northwestern Europe.'"

"Crumpets and tea, anyone?" Janice laughed. "You're a Brit like me, Tess!"

"Partly." She scanned the page. "But check this out. 'Twenty-four percent Ireland and Scotland.'"

"Kick up yer heels, lassie!" LuAnn said. "Yer Scottish, like me!"

"Partly, but look at this. I'm fifteen percent Germanic European." Tess pointed at the screen.

"I think we've safely established that you're European." Janice giggled. "No one can argue that point. So far there are no big surprises."

Tess opened the DNA Matches folder to see what surprises lay in store. "Wow, I have a lot of cousins."

"Right. You always find more than you bargained for in the cousin department," Janice explained.

Tess scrolled the pages and tried to piece things together. "I recognize a few of the screen names of my first and second cousins. But when we get back as far as fourth and fifth cousins, I'm as lost as a goose. Who knew I had so many of them active on the ancestry site?"

A noise in the lobby startled them, and Tess jumped. "Oh my. I think I'm nervous."

Janice stuck her head out the door and then said, "It's Reena and Richard. They've just come back down to the lobby."

"Ah." Tess was too preoccupied with the test results to think about Richard and Reena. "I don't know if I told you ladies, but I actually took this test because there's been a rumor in our family for ages that the man everyone always *thought* was my great-grandfather really wasn't. According to family rumors, the real whodunit was a fellow with the last name of Atkinson."

"So, take a look at your matches and see if you see any Atkinsons in there."

Tess scrolled for a few moments and gasped as the truth came into view. "Oh my goodness." She turned back to look at her friends. "I'm an Atkinson, through and through! The rumor wasn't a rumor. It was true!" She pointed at the screen. "Look at all of these matches. Wow! I've got a whole other side to my family that I knew nothing about."

Janice leaned over to have a closer look. "Wow, that's remarkable."

Tess kept browsing her cousins list until she came upon a screen name that looked familiar. *RNewberry.*

"Wait. RNewberry? Do you think there's any chance that could be...?" She clicked the link, and a family tree opened. Unfortunately, she didn't learn much from it, because it was listed as private. Tess turned to face LuAnn. "Do me a favor?"

"Of course."

"Go get Reena. I've got to find out if this is just a fluke."

Less than a minute later, Reena entered the room with Richard directly behind her. "What's going on in here? Is the building on fire?"

"No." Tess leaned forward in her chair. "You did your DNA test, right?"

"Yes, of course. I'm quite the historian, if I do say so myself." She gave Tess an inquisitive look. "Oh, is that what this is about? You got your results?"

"Yes, and they're a little...shocking."

"Why is that?"

Tess pointed at the screen. It took a minute for Reena to catch on, but when she did, she started to squeal. "What's this I see? You're an Atkinson?"

"Keep looking." She pointed at the link to RNewberry's family tree, and Reena gasped.

"Oh my goodness, Tess! We're related on the Atkinson side. We're kin!" Reena threw her arms around Tess's neck and hollered, "Hello, Cousin!"

# CHAPTER FIFTEEN

*April 7ᵗʰ, 1862*

Prudence spent the next couple of days caring for Nate and Jack. The dog's wound showed signs of healing, but Nate's shoulder continued to fester. She wondered if the injury might be more than she could handle without a doctor's care, so she sent for Doc Fredericks. He came at once.

The good doctor examined their patient but shared his concerns privately with Prudence and Jason. "I fear the infection has become too great," he said. "And his fever might prove to be his undoing. I sincerely doubt the young man will survive more than a few days, at best. I will send a message to his division, so someone can come to transport his body home once he passes away."

The very idea broke Prudence's heart.

Jack stayed at Nate's bedside, a loyal and faithful companion. He seemed to sense the man's needs, even before they were voiced.

Prudence and Jason prayed diligently for the young man. As she and Jason settled into bed that night, she shared her concerns that Nate would not survive. Jason pulled her close and whispered words of comfort. "Do not let fear consume thee, Pru."

"I cannot dare to hope that he will survive." Even as she spoke the word *hope* her heart flinched. Her thoughts shifted back to little Hope, her precious daughter. She had only survived a few minutes of this life, though Prudence had prayed fervently for her.

Did God still answer prayers for the healing of His children? Could He—would He—touch Nate while there was still time? Prudence tossed and turned in the bed, more worried than ever.

# Chapter Sixteen

"Hello, Cousin!" Tess laughed as the realization set in. "Who knew?"

"Now that I think about it..." Reena gazed at her with greater intensity than before. "You've got a lot of the Atkinson features."

"And I do love a good cup of tea."

"Me too! Let's have a cup right now, and I'll bring you up to speed on the other cousins. But first I have to find out our common ancestor. Do you mind?"

"Of course not."

Tess scooted over, and Reena took the seat. She scrolled around on Tess's family tree until she came upon someone she seemed to know. "Voilà! Here she is, my great-grandmother, Birdie Atkinson." Reena pointed at the screen.

"Wait, Birdie Atkinson?" Tess paused to think it through. "Why does that name sound so familiar?"

"Because I mentioned her so many times when I stayed with you last year. She's the one whose beau sent a message up north, and Prudence baked the ring into the bread. Remember?" Reena stuck out her hand and showed off the delicate little ring.

"The ring! Of course." Tess shook her head. "I just can't get over it. You'll have to explain how all of the puzzle pieces fit later, but for now it's good enough to know I'm related to you."

"So, Atkinson is a British name?" Janice asked.

Reena nodded. "Oh yes. We trace our Atkinson name back to the 1500s. Let me show you."

She signed out of Tess's ancestry account and then signed back in under her own account. Minutes later, a whole new world opened up. Tess could hardly believe the amount of work Reena had put into tracing her family so many generations.

"As you can see, we trace our lineage back to a man named Guyot Atkinson, who was born in the year 1520 in Yorkshire, England."

LuAnn leaned against the edge of the desk. "Well, I'll be. I had no idea you could go that far back."

"When your family has a history as rich as ours, you sure can." Reena beamed with pride. "Oh, Tess, we're going to have such a fun time making these discoveries. I'm so glad we can stay in touch through the internet. I've got all sorts of documents to share with you."

"Thank you," Tess responded, her heart overflowing. "This is all so fascinating."

"And to think, we were just talking about DNA testing for dogs." Janice laughed. "Who knew we'd end up tracing your family back hundreds of years, Tess."

"Are you ladies thinking about having Huck's DNA tested?" Reena asked.

"Oh, no. Actually…" Tess paused, not knowing how much, if any, of Geneva's story to share. "Another dog altogether. We were just discussing the fact that many are testing their dogs to prove their lineage."

Andy Lawson popped his head in the door. "What's going on in here? Some kind of party?"

"Sort of." Reena giggled. "Tess and I just found out that we're cousins."

"Distant cousins," Tess explained as she peered over Reena's shoulder at the computer screen. "If this website can be believed. But we're cousins, nonetheless."

"Well, congratulations." He gave them a broad smile. "That's a wonderful revelation."

"Indeed." Tess hated to dampen the mood but felt led to ask about Jelly. "Have you heard anything?"

"Still no word, but we're not giving up yet. We decided to put up a Facebook page about Jelly so people can help us search. Otherwise I'll feel awful leaving Marietta on Sunday morning if she's not with us. At least this way we'll feel like we're actually doing something."

"Send me a link to the page," Janice said. "I can share it on my profile page, and maybe others will do the same."

"Yes, I want to see it too," Reena said. "To be honest, I barely remember what your little girl looks like. I only saw her that first day."

"Oh, I've got dozens of pictures." Andy scrolled through his phone until he found several. "Here's one of Callie and Jelly Bean at the park last summer. And here's one of Jelly chasing

Wyatt around the bases at the baseball field. I've always loved that one."

"She's a beautiful spaniel," Richard observed as he glanced at the phone.

"Yes, she is." Reena's voice cracked. "Sorry, I'm just so sad for the kids. And for you. It breaks my heart to think that they might never see her—" She stopped short of saying it. "Well, it breaks my heart."

"Thank you. I'm pretty heartbroken too. I never dreamed I'd care this much about a dog, but Jelly is as important to us as any of our other friends. She's a part of us."

"Of course." Reena and Richard spoke in unison.

"Here's the page we put up." Andy showed them the app on his phone. "We chose our favorite pictures of her—in the ring and out."

"If you'll email us that link, I'll share it right away," Tess said.

"Me too," LuAnn agreed. "Just send it to the inn's email address, and we'll do what we can."

Andy fidgeted with his phone and then looked up and said, "Done. It's in your email. We appreciate your help trying to find our little girl. Speaking of little girls, I'd better get upstairs and help Tandi put the kids to bed. Callie was exhausted. We had a long day."

"Did the kids enjoy the agility events?" LuAnn asked.

He nodded. "Oh, they loved it. It was the best distraction."

"And tomorrow? What will you do?"

He shrugged. "I think we'll just stay put here. It would hurt too much to show up at the event. And if Jelly isn't in the ring at the appointed time, the runner-up will take her place." He paused. "It's just better not to be there, I think. Less painful for everyone involved."

"I understand." Tess felt compelled to share something else though. "Andy, I want you to know that I'm praying for your family and for Jelly. I know some people might think it's silly to pray for a dog—I might've been one of them a few days back, actually—but I'm happy to pray for her."

"Oh, I am too," Reena said. "I believe that God cares about all of the creatures He created. If He cares about them, then why wouldn't we pray for them?"

"We're grateful for those prayers," Andy said. "And like I said before, we haven't given up. We won't, either. We'll keep on hoping."

He wished them good night and then turned and walked up the stairs.

"Aren't they the sweetest family ever?" Janice asked after he was out of earshot. "I just think they're wonderful."

"Such a shame that a family that sweet would lose someone who means so much to them. It breaks my heart."

Reena grew quiet, which was unusual for her.

"Earth to Reena," Richard said after a moment. "A penny for your thoughts."

"Yes, what has you so deep in thought?" Tess asked.

Reena seemed to snap to attention. "Oh, sorry. I was just thinking about the pictures he showed us on his phone. Their dog reminds me of that little spaniel we took in a couple of days back, the one that's still on the bus. I love to see dogs with such beautiful coloring and luscious fur. Black and white were just meant to go together."

"There's a black-and-white cocker spaniel on the Paws on Wheels bus?" Tess's heart quickened. "Are you sure?"

"Well, pretty sure. It's that dog Jordan told us about, the one that the owner surrendered here in the Marietta area."

"Sure, I remember the leftover dog on the bus, but no one told me it was a black-and-white cocker spaniel." Tess paced the room. "Why wouldn't Jordan have mentioned that? He knows there's a missing dog that matches that description. It's got to be more than a coincidence."

Reena's eyes widened. "Oh, you don't think…"

"It's got to be her. But there's only one way we'll know for sure." Tess turned to face Reena. "Reena, it's up to you. Jordan trusts you. Would you be willing to go onto that bus and check that last crate to see if it's Angelica? You've seen her picture. You know what she looks like."

"I—I—" Reena paled. "Okay, I'll do it."

"Just act normal, okay? Don't let him know you're concerned."

"He's going to wonder why I'm going back on the bus though." She snapped her fingers. "Oh, I know! I could tell him that I want pictures of the dog to share with my dog-loving friends. If it turns out to be a different doggie, she'll need a new home, after all."

"True, but what if he and Missy are sleeping already?" Tess asked.

"It's only nine o'clock. I doubt they're asleep." Reena shifted her gaze to Richard. "Do you feel up to driving to the arena, Richard?"

His gaze drifted to the floor. "I'm not so sure. My vision's not so good at night." He rubbed his eyes, and for the first time, Tess noticed how red-rimmed they were.

"That's okay," Tess said. "I'll drive."

Less than ten minutes later they were in her Honda, headed to the arena. Tess's pulse thumped in her ears as she thought about what they were about to do. Was it possible Jelly had been this close all along? Oh, why hadn't she given all those crates a closer look when she was on the bus? Surely she would have noticed the dog then, and this drama would be over.

As they drove, LuAnn peppered Tess with questions. "What if Jordan is armed? What if he gets angry? Shouldn't we call the police?"

"Let's wait and see how he responds," Tess suggested. "If things go south, we can always call for backup. For now, let's just stay calm and act like we're simply dropping in on old friends."

"I just don't know what to think about all of this," Reena said. "I'm so disappointed in Jordan, if this is all true. I really believed that he cared about dogs. Why would he steal one?"

"Maybe someone else put him up to it," Richard suggested. "You know what I mean? Maybe someone—one of the competitors—brought the dog to Jordan and claimed it was a family member's dog. Maybe he didn't realize it was the missing dog. That would explain it, right?"

"Yes, that would explain it." Tess pulled her car into the parking lot of the arena but kept a little distance between herself and the Paws on Wheels bus. "Let's give him the benefit of the doubt."

When the vehicle stopped, Reena opened the back door and climbed out.

"You're going alone over my dead body." Richard got out and slipped his arm over her shoulders. "We're doing this as a team."

"Thank you, Richard." She reached up and gave him a little kiss on the cheek. "My knight in shining armor."

"I haven't been called that in years," he said. "And just for the record, my knees are knocking right now. I'm not exactly knight material. And the only thing shining about me is the bald spot on the back of my head."

Reena's eyelashes fluttered as she said, "You're plenty good enough for me. And don't worry. I'll ask to take pictures of the dog to share. Jordan won't even be suspicious."

Tess and LuAnn stayed seated in the car, watching closely as Reena and Richard walked toward the bus. Under her breath, Tess offered up a hasty prayer that God would protect them.

Seconds later, Jordan opened the door of the bus, and Reena and Richard climbed inside. Several minutes went by and nothing happened.

From the back seat, Janice muttered, "What's taking so long?"

Tess was wondering the very same thing. "I hope Jordan isn't giving her a hard time. You don't think so, do you? I mean, do you think he's dangerous? Oh, maybe one of us should have gone instead."

A few minutes later, Reena and Richard stepped down from the bus. Tess and the other ladies spilled out of the car and met them in the parking lot.

"Well?" Tess asked.

Reena waved her phone. "He let me in, no questions asked. And I got pictures of the dog too. Check this one out." She brought up the first picture. "Well, pooh. Looks like I only got its head in this photo. But look. It's a black-and-white spaniel, all right. Really sweet too, but kind of squirmy."

"The lighting's not very good." Janice took the phone and pulled it close to give the picture another glance. "Did you get any more photos? Anything clearer than this?"

"Yes." Reena fiddled with her phone once again until she came up with a photograph that seemed a little more focused. "Poor little baby was tired of being cooped up in that crate. She wouldn't sit still for a photo op."

"Sounds like Jelly," LuAnn said. "She's a feisty one, all right."

Reena pointed at the picture. "There you go, ladies. One black-and-white cocker spaniel."

The picture looked a little blurry to Tess, but seeing the dog in the photo stirred her to action. "Okay, so what do we do now?"

"I say we call the police to let them know we've found Jelly. I won't call Andy until the police have Jelly in their possession." LuAnn made the call, and minutes later, a police car pulled up, lights flashing and siren screaming.

Jordan—likely frightened by the noise—opened the door of the bus and stuck his head out. The officer got out of the driver's seat and approached Jordan, shining a flashlight in his face.

"Whoa!" Jordan put his hands over his eyes. "What in the world?"

"I got a call about a stolen dog?" The officer sounded as confused as he looked.

"Yes." Tess took a few steps closer and pointed to Jordan. "She's on the bus."

"Wait, what?" Jordan stepped down onto the pavement. "*Stolen* dog?"

Reena nodded. "Yes, but you already know that, don't you, Jordan?"

"Know what?" He looked genuinely perplexed.

"Why, Jordan?" Reena asked. "What were you planning to do with her?"

"Do with her? Who's *her*?" He shook his head.

The officer put his hand up. "Could someone fill me in? I'm a little confused about why I'm here. I just heard that a missing dog had been found."

"That's right." Tess shared the story. "We've been hot on the trail of a certain cocker spaniel who was stolen a couple of days back. Now we've found her. She's on that bus. We have the photos to prove it."

"The dog on my bus was stolen?" Jordan's eyes widened. "Whoa. Hold up. I met the owner's daughter a couple of days ago. She surrendered the dog because her mom passed away.

The whole story was pretty heartbreaking, but it didn't involve any sort of theft. Not to my knowledge, anyway."

"You can cut the act, Jordan." Reena planted her hands on her hips. "We know you have Jelly on this bus."

"Jelly?" He ran his fingers through his hair, and his eyes narrowed. "Are you talking about that missing cocker spaniel, from the dog show?"

"Yes," Reena said. "I saw you put a black-and-white cocker spaniel on this bus the very day Jelly went missing."

His eyes clouded over. "Oh…"

"Yes, though I'm stunned, Jordan." Reena's voice elevated in pitch. "How in the world did this happen?"

"How did I end up with the dog on the bus, you mean?"

"I know you don't agree with pedigree dogs," Reena said, "but have you met the Lawsons? Do you see how they've grieved over this dog? Those children are brokenhearted. Their mother is beside herself. And I've rarely seen a grown man cry, but Andy has been shattered by this dog's loss. And all of it because of you." Reena poked her index finger into his chest.

"All because of me. Right." He pointed to the door of the bus. "Follow me, please."

The police officer cleared his throat. "Someone want to include me in this little adventure?"

"Officer, you first." Jordan gestured for them to join him as he climbed on board.

Tess stepped up onto the bus and followed behind Jordan and the others to a crate at the very back. He opened it and reached inside to pull the little dog out. Tess gasped as she laid eyes on the pooch. Poor little Jelly. She'd put on a lot of weight over the past few days, hadn't she? And so much for the beautiful grooming job. Her fur looked completely different.

"Oh, you poor little thing!" She reached out to pet the dog. "Someone mistreated you."

"No, someone overfed this old girl," Jordan said. "Over a period of several years, I'd say."

"Overfed?" Tess, Janice, and LuAnn asked in unison.

"Mm-hmm." He held the dog up. "Folks, I'd like to introduce you to Princess Penelope from Marietta, Ohio."

"Princess Penelope?" They all spoke in unison.

"Yes, she's a nine-year-old *King Charles Cavalier* spaniel, surrendered—as I said—by her former owner's daughter after the owner passed away. The owner overfed her, as you can tell by looking at her somewhat tubby physique."

"Oy vey," was all Tess could think to say.

"I thought we had a forever family for her, but they backed out at the last minute, so this little girl is still looking for a home." He turned to face Richard. "I actually thought you were interested."

"She is pretty cute." Richard reached over to scratch her behind the ears. "I think Schmaltzy would like her."

"At this point, I'm not sure I'd give one of our dogs to any of you." He set the dog down on the floor of the bus. "But I will find a home for her. I'm not too worried about that. Lots of people are on the lookout for King Charles spaniels. They're very expensive." He shook his head. "I wouldn't be surprised to hear that the former owner paid close to two thousand dollars for this little girl nine years ago."

"I guess King Charles spaniels resemble cockers, right?" Reena asked. "I wasn't *too* far off."

"Right. But I can assure you, this isn't the dog everyone is looking for."

"Well, if this isn't Jelly, then where is she?" Richard asked.

"I have no idea," Jordan said. "But just for the record, I would *never* hurt a dog. I care about all dogs, mutt or pedigree. I don't discriminate, despite what you might have read in that article Winston wrote a few years ago." He gave Reena a look of disbelief. "And you, Reena? Really? I'm shocked that you suspected me after all the time we've spent together. I thought you knew me better than that."

"I'm sorry, Jordan." She released an exaggerated sigh. "I think I just got caught up in the moment. It almost felt like I was in one of those TV mysteries."

"It's all my fault," Tess said. "I put two and two together and came up with what I thought was four."

"So, we don't have a stolen dog on this bus?" The officer leaned against the row of crates. "Am I hearing that right?"

"You're hearing that right," Jordan said.

"She's kind of a sweet old dog, though." The officer knelt down and scratched the pooch behind the ears. "My mom loves spaniels. We always had one in the house when I was growing up. She's all alone in her condo since my dad died last fall."

"Really?" Jordan smiled. "Well, why don't you leave your information? After Princess Penelope is given a clean bill of health, I'll be in touch to see if your mom is interested."

"I'd like that." The officer leaned forward to give the pup a kiss on the top of the head. "I'd have to say this was a divine appointment, wouldn't you?"

Jordan looked like he wasn't as sure. And Tess? Well, she felt like a total goober for jumping to conclusions.

# CHAPTER SEVENTEEN

N o one said much on the trip back to the inn. Tess felt particularly sorry for Reena and finally managed an apology.

"I hope this doesn't damage your friendship with Jordan and Missy."

"I don't think it will. Jordan's got a pretty good sense of humor. Maybe tomorrow he'll laugh at all of this."

"Laugh that we dragged him out of his home on wheels so a police officer could confront him about a dog he'd supposedly stolen?" Richard asked. "Or laugh that we actually thought he was capable of dognapping?"

"Well, when you put it like that…" Reena chuckled. "Actually, I'm not worried about it. Right now, I just need to get a good night's sleep. My thoughts will be clearer in the morning. I'll be better able to offer an apology then."

"Are you planning to go to the Best in Show tomorrow?" Richard asked Tess. "That round begins at eleven o'clock."

"I don't know." Right now, Tess just wanted to crawl into bed and pull the covers over her head. Besides, what if she showed up to the event and Jordan was there? She couldn't face him again.

They arrived back at the inn just after ten. Richard got onto the elevator with Reena but then pushed the button to stop the door from closing.

"Tess?" he called out.

"Yes?"

"I meant to tell you this earlier but forgot. You know how I've been looking for that article Winston wrote about the dog who called 911?"

"Right. You've been eager for me to read it."

"There's no point now," he said. "It turns out, it's not true."

"What?" Tess, LuAnn, and Reena spoke in unison.

The elevator door tried to close, but Richard stopped it with another press of the button. "Yes, the paper actually recanted that story and several others he wrote for them. Turns out, he was fabricating his dog tales to grow his readership and to ensure his place at the magazine."

"What? Are you sure?"

"Yes. I went straight to the source. I called the *Canine Companion* this afternoon to ask if they could mail a copy of that issue to you, Tess. But when I mentioned the particulars of the story, I was given quite an earful."

"That's crazy," Reena said. "Why would he do that?"

"Who knows?" Richard shrugged. "Sensationalism? Point is, he made it all up and got caught."

"That's nuts," LuAnn said and then yawned. "Anything for a story, eh?"

"Maybe." Tess paused to think it through. "But I would think in an environment like the dog show he'd find stories aplenty. Why make them up?"

"To garner attention?" LuAnn suggested. "Fame?"

"Crazy." Tess still couldn't believe it. "What kind of person goes to such extremes to make a name for himself?"

"Anyway, just thought you'd want to know." Richard let the door shut, and the gentle hum of the elevator kicked in.

As Tess and LuAnn climbed the stairs, they heard crying coming from the second floor where the Lawson children were supposed to be sleeping. They paused long enough to hear Tandi comforting her daughter. The poor little girl was in so much anguish over losing her sweet Angelica. Who could blame her for weeping?

It seemed everyone was feeling this loss keenly. Tess couldn't remember the last time so many people had been affected by one animal.

When they reached the fourth floor she said good night to LuAnn then headed to her room. Tess glanced down and realized Huck was still with her.

"You sweet old boy." She leaned down and scratched him behind the ears. "You're a permanent fixture in our world, and I wouldn't change that for anything."

He lagged behind her as she entered her room and then, once she closed the door, he curled up in the corner. By the time she turned down the covers, the pooch was snoring peacefully.

Tess brushed her teeth and changed into her pjs. As she set her phone on the bedside table, a notification popped up. Only then did she realize she'd missed a call from Winnie. Tess checked the voice mail. Winnie's message was simple. "I'll see you in the morning at the usual time." At least that's what Tess thought she said. The sound of a dog barking in the background made her message a little hard to hear. As she climbed into bed and pulled the covers up, she thought through the events of the day. Jelly was still missing. And, while she didn't have a clear picture of who might have taken her, it was becoming clearer who had not. Geneva was surely not to blame. She was far too preoccupied with her own troubles. And Jordan hadn't taken her either. If Randy was right, video footage proved that Russ Schumer had stayed put at his grooming station. Even if he had some sort of bitterness toward the Lawson family, he would never risk his reputation to get even with them. That much was evident.

At this point, Tess had to wonder if, perhaps, the little dog really had just run off of her own accord. Maybe she would still turn up in one of the local shelters.

Or maybe…

Tess sat up in the bed, an idea hitting like a bolt of lightning. Of all the rabbit trails she'd gone down, there was one she still hadn't followed to the end. She reached for her laptop and opened it. Her hands trembled as she went straight to the ancestry site. Once there, she dug right in, researching the only person who still felt like a suspect to her—Winston James.

Huck must have sensed her anxiety. He rose and came to the side of the bed, resting his head against the sheets. She reached down and petted his head. "I think I'm onto something, boy. We're gonna find that little Jelly Bean if we have to stay up all night to do it."

When a knock sounded at her bedroom door around midnight, Tess nearly came out of her skin. Who else was up at this hour?

"Tess?" LuAnn's voice sounded from outside her door. "Are you still awake in there?"

"Yes." She steadied her breathing. "Come on in."

LuAnn pushed the door open then took a couple of steps inside her room. "I thought I saw your light. I got up because this little guy here"—she indicated Tom, their resident cat and Huck's best friend—"was looking for Huck." She walked over and sat on the edge of Tess's bed. "Why are you still up?"

"I couldn't sleep. I've been on a quest to see if Winston really has an ex-wife. Remember how he said she was at the competition showing the dog?"

"Yes."

"Well, I didn't see her."

"Neither did I."

"He brought up his ex again when he came to the inn. I asked him how the dog had fared in the competition, and the conversation got rather twisted."

"What did he say?"

"He seemed flustered, couldn't seem to come up with an answer. Something about the way he reacted raised red flags, so I decided to look him up online. You know how I've been researching my family tree?"

"Of course. You're not going to tell me Winston James is your cousin too, are you? Or maybe he's Reena's long-lost grandson? Something like that?" LuAnn grinned.

"No, silly. But, I got to thinking about how much information is out there on that site. You can find out a lot about people there, and not just relatives. For instance, you can look up birth records, divorces, marriage licenses, and so on—for anyone you like."

"Right." LuAnn nodded.

"So that's what I did. I had to guess at his age but finally located the right Winston James. I mean, it must be him, because I found a record of a marriage and subsequent divorce to a woman named Marigold O'Ryan."

"So, the ex-wife story is true, which means it's possible the story about Horace is true too. And he said his wife was with her dog in the family area at the arena?"

"Yes."

"What was his dog's name, do you remember?"

"Horace."

LuAnn sat up a little straighter. "Hey, I know. Let's look up the dogs who competed and see if we can find a dog with that name."

"Good idea." Tess searched until she located the Marietta *Canine Companion* competition site. She browsed event after event but couldn't find the name Horace anywhere, or any variation of it.

"Nothing." Tess looked up from the laptop. "There's no Horace listed."

"What? Are you sure?"

"But Winston had that crate—he said he was taking Horace to compete. That makes no sense at all. Unless…" Tess snapped her fingers. "LuAnn, that's it! He brought a crate into the arena, and he carried that same crate out of the arena hours later."

"Didn't everyone?"

"Yes, but you're missing my point. What if he carried in the empty crate under the guise of entering the competition, then left with another dog inside of it? I can see how he might have done that. And, if so, it explains the blanket on top. Maybe it really was Jelly inside that crate when he waltzed out of the building!"

"Tess, I don't know. Remember what happened just last night with Jordan. You let your imagination run away with you, and we ended up falsely accusing him. You don't want to do the same thing to someone else. This story sounds pretty far-fetched, if you think about it."

"Maybe."

"What are you going to do?" LuAnn asked.

"I'm going to call the police and then leave the rest up to them. I still don't know for sure that Winston has the dog, but I do know that he'll show up at the event tomorrow because he's hungry for a story. The police will be able to arrest him there."

"If he stole the dog, which we still can't prove."

"Right." She sighed. "I haven't quite figured out how to prove that. Hey, maybe he'll return Jelly at the last minute! Wouldn't that be something?"

LuAnn shrugged. "I think you're tired. Either that, or your imagination has kicked into overdrive. You need sleep, Tess. But call the police first to let them know about the ex-wife and about Horace. That way you really can leave it up to them."

When LuAnn left the room, Tess reached for her cell phone. She made a quick call to the Marietta Police Department and left a message for Randy. Hopefully he would get it before tomorrow morning's big event.

Tess fell into a fitful sleep and awoke several hours later feeling awful. Her neck was stiff, and her head ached. As she lay in the bed, she began to question everything—her decision to call the police, how she'd accused Jordan—all of it. She began to pray in earnest that God would take control of this situation, not for her sake, but for Callie's and Wyatt's. They needed their friend back, and only the Lord knew how to accomplish that.

Tess showered and dressed, then took a couple of Tylenol before going downstairs. The last thing she felt like doing was helping in the kitchen, but their guests needed a hearty breakfast this morning before the big event.

Before she made it to the kitchen, Tess ran into Geneva coming out of her room with Gigi. They were both dressed in a lime-green and hot-pink ensemble. She stopped in the hallway to chat.

Geneva was bubbling with excitement. "Tess, you'll never believe what happened! I went to that boutique, the one you told me about. Antoinette's Closet. Great place."

"See? I knew you would love it."

"I did. Emma's so sweet and has a great eye for what's trending, clothes-wise." Geneva wrinkled her nose. "But she had absolutely nothing for dogs at all. So I convinced her to let me send some of my samples to her."

"You make your own dog outfits?"

"Sure do." She pointed at her jumpsuit. "When I buy a new outfit for myself I go straight to the fabric store and buy something similar for Gigi."

"I never would have guessed that her clothes were homemade."

"I've learned a lot over the years. I think I've got a pretty good eye."

"Pretty good? You're remarkable, Geneva."

"Thanks." Her cheeks flushed pink. "So, here's what she agreed to do. When she takes in a new line of clothes she's going to send me pictures, and I'll put together some matching outfits. Before long, all of the ladies in town will look like their best friends."

"And by best friends, I'm assuming you mean their dogs?"

"Well, of course." She pointed at Huck. "And since we're talking about dogs, I've been meaning to tell you that Huck would look amazing in a little tuxedo with tails. If you have a big event coming up, I mean."

Tess bit her tongue before saying, "We'll pass." Instead, she just smiled. "Well now, wouldn't that be something? Huck the Wonder Dog, all duded up with no place to go."

"He might catch the eye of a pretty little lady if he plays the part well."

Okay, this was just getting weird. Time to change the subject.

"Well, I'm glad things went well with Emma. Are you headed back up to the arena today?"

Geneva frowned. "Yeah, but not to compete. I'll fill you in on all of that later, I promise. Thanks again for suggesting the boutique."

"You're welcome." Tess headed downstairs, completely delighted that Geneva was in better spirits today. When she got to the kitchen, Tess found Winnie up to her elbows in cinnamon rolls.

"My goodness, you must have gotten here early," she commented. "That dough has already risen."

"Yes, I've been here a couple of hours. I went to bed early but was still up most of the night."

"Because of your neighbor's dog?"

"Yes." Winnie stopped loading the cinnamon rolls onto the tray and looked Tess's way. "Hey, I just realized why that man looks so familiar."

"What man?"

"The one who keeps showing up like he's one of our guests and sitting in the café for hours at a time. The one who annoys me to no end."

"Do you mean Winston James?"

"Yes. He grates on me. I've never met anyone who marched right into a place and made himself at home like that. And to think, he's not even a guest at Wayfarers!"

"Why does he look familiar?"

Winnie situated the cinnamon rolls and gave them a solid once-over before popping them into the oven. "I think he's the one who rented my neighbor's cottage for the week. I saw him getting into his car this morning."

"Wait—what?"

"Pretty sure it was him getting into that fancy sports car." She closed the oven door and set the timer. "But I don't think he took his dog with him, which means that yappy little thing will be there all day, annoying the neighbors. Why do people do that...leave dogs to annoy everyone in the neighborhood?"

"Are you sure he left a dog in the house?"

"Of course. I heard barking after he left." Winnie turned her attention to the dirty dishes. "That's why I'm glad to be here and not at home. At least here I can have some peace and quiet."

From the living room, Gigi took to barking.

Winnie laughed. "Well, a little peace and quiet, anyway."

"Thank you for telling me, Winnie. The plot thickens."

"Plot? Hmm?"

"Either Horace is very real and hanging out at the cottage next door to you, or you have just answered the question of who stole Angelica."

"I did that?" Winnie looked up from a sink full of dirty dishes. "Go figure. And all I wanted was a good night's sleep."

# CHAPTER EIGHTEEN

Just as Tess reached for her cell phone to call Randy, her phone rang. She recognized his voice on the other end of the line.

"Tess? It's Randy. Thanks for the tip about Winston James. He's been a person of interest in this case for days now."

"Really?"

"Yes. We caught some footage of him leaving the arena with a dog crate, which we found strange, since he's there as a freelanc writer, not a competitor. He claimed his ex-wife's dog was inside."

"You mean Horace?"

"Yes, but when I contacted the registrar at the event, I was told there was no Horace entered, just like you said in your message."

"Well, hold on to your hat," she said. "I have even more information now, and I think you'll be very interested to hear it." She shared what she'd learned from Winnie, and moments later Randy was en route to Winnie's neighbor's cottage. They finalized a plan of action, agreeing to meet at the security station in the arena, then Tess ended the call. There was no time to waste.

Janice met up with her in the lobby. "Where are you going in such a hurry? And by the way, your blouse is inside out."

"What?" Tess scurried into the office, closed the door, and adjusted her blouse. When she reemerged, Janice was still standing in the same spot, arms crossed.

"Would you mind telling me what's going on?"

"I'm sorry to leave in such a hurry, Janice, but I've got to get up to the arena to meet Randy. I think we've located Jelly."

"You've located Jelly?" These words came from Andy as he descended the stairs from the second floor. "Where? Is she okay? Are you sure it's her?"

*Ack.* She hadn't meant to alert the family until she knew for sure.

Tess glanced up at him. "Andy, I think Winston James has Jelly at the cottage he's renting, which happens to be next door to Winnie's place."

"Winston James? Really?" He stopped on the stair in front of her. "Why in the world would he…? Never mind." The pitch of his voice rose as his face reddened. "Where is it? Give me the address."

"No, let's not handle it that way. I've already called the police, and they are on their way to check it out. I don't think it's safe for you to go there. Officer Lewis promised to bring the dog up to the arena if, indeed, there is a dog at the cottage. None of this is certain yet. It's just a hunch, but an educated one. I'm very hopeful."

He nodded. "Okay. Tandi and I will get the kids dressed. We'll meet you at the arena, Tess. And thank you for staying on top of this for us. We're very grateful to have you on our side." He corrected himself. "On *Jelly's* side."

"You're more than welcome. I pray I'm right, Andy. I want this story to have a happy ending."

"Me too. You have no idea how badly I want that—for the kids, for Tandi, and for me."

Tess swapped phone numbers with him and then watched as he bounded up the stairs, two at a time.

She headed out the door to the arena and hit every red light along the way. Why did it always seem to happen like that when she was in a hurry?

Tess arrived fifteen minutes later to a near-empty arena parking lot. She looked around for a patrol car but didn't see one. Locating a spot near the front door wasn't hard to do, considering, but she was hesitant to go inside until she saw Randy's patrol car.

Then she happened to see Russ Schumer getting out of the van next to her, and she sprang into action. Tess managed to catch up with him about halfway to the arena door.

"Mr. Schumer, wait!"

He turned and frowned when he saw her. "Yes?"

"I need to ask you a question." She rested her hand on her throat as she attempted to catch her breath. "Did you groom a dog named Horace a few days back?"

"Horace?" Creases formed between his eyes. "That name doesn't sound familiar."

"Do you know Winston James, the reporter?"

"Know him?" He snorted. "Who doesn't? That guy tried to wreck my career a few years ago. He's always trying to sniff out a story, one that puts him in the best light and the subject in the worst. I don't trust him as far as I can throw him. Trust me when I say that I send him packing whenever he comes my way. Everyone does."

"He told me that he and his ex-wife have a dog that competed and that you groomed him just before."

Russ shrugged. "I never knew he had a dog, and I certainly never groomed one for him."

"Thank you. You've helped—a lot."

"You're welcome." He opened the door, and she walked inside. The puzzle pieces were coming together. She ushered up a quick prayer for Randy and his team, then headed for the security area. Along the way, she happened upon Winston in the snack bar, drinking a cup of coffee. Not wanting to alert him to anything, she simply waved and kept walking.

"You're here early," he called out.

"Yes, I..." She hesitated. "I'm meeting a friend." She prayed he wouldn't follow her, and he did not. It didn't take long to reach the security area. Less than five minutes later, the Lawson family arrived.

"Any word from the police?" Andy asked.

"No, not yet. I—" Her phone rang, and she nearly dropped it when she saw Randy's number appear on the screen. One rushed, "Hello?" later, she received the news they had all been waiting for.

"We've got her!" Randy's voice teemed with excitement. "We've got Angelica. She's in good shape and was very happy to see us. We're just outside the arena, about to head inside with her."

"Oh, that's wonderful news!" Tess did her best not to squeal aloud as her emotions took over.

"We're on our way up to the arena now to nab Winston James. Thanks so much for your work on this, Tess."

"You're welcome. Can I pass the phone to Andy Lawson so you can tell him personally?"

"Please do."

Andy took the phone and, seconds later, his eyes filled with tears. He nodded in his wife's direction, and she too started crying.

"Mommy, what's wrong?" Callie tugged at her mom's blouse.

"Nothing, honey." Tandi scooped her daughter into her arms. "The police officer just told Daddy that he found Jelly. They're bringing her to us now."

"He found Jelly?" Callie and Wyatt hollered in unison.

Tandi nodded with tears flowing down her cheeks.

Only then did Tess realize that Winston had joined them. He paled and turned to run, but ran smack-dab into Russ Schumer, who was loaded down with grooming gear. Winston's backpack hit the floor, and he tripped over it as he attempted to flee.

"Stop him, Russ!" Andy called out. "He stole Angelica!"

As Winston scrambled up from the floor, Russ went into action. He grabbed him by the arm and held him firmly in place. "Oh, no you don't."

Andy gave Tess's phone back to her and raced to help Russ contain Winston.

"What's this about?" Winston pulled against their tight hold. "You can't do this to me."

"We can and we will."

They didn't have to hold him long. Randy arrived a couple of minutes later with Jelly on a leash. The dog bolted toward Tandi and the kids, and they all began to cry and shout at once.

The good officer flew into action, handcuffing Winston. He read him his Miranda rights and then gestured for him to take a seat in a nearby chair.

"I haven't done anything wrong!" Winston hollered.

"We located Angelica at the home you're renting, Mr. James." Randy gave him a warning look. "I would advise you not to speak until you've acquired an attorney."

"I don't need an attorney, I'm telling you. I didn't take that dog. I don't know how she wandered into my house, but I didn't take her."

"I'll tell you exactly how you did it." Tess stepped up to him. "On Wednesday, after Angelica won Best in Breed, you made your way into the family lounge under the pretense of visiting your ex-wife and her dog, Horace. Instead, you waited for your opportunity to nab Jelly and place her in a crate you had brought into the arena earlier in the day. You draped a blanket over the crate to conceal her whereabouts."

Winston flinched.

"If you wanted to hurt our family, you got your wish." Tandi wagged her finger in the man's face. "But if you think you're going to turn our little doll into a money-making story for some magazine, you've got another think coming."

"Trust me, there's not a magazine in the country that will take an article from him now, unless it's one detailing his penchant for crime." Randy instructed Winston to stand.

After a few more questions, Randy escorted Winston out of the building. The Lawsons were so busy doting on Jelly that they almost forgot about the upcoming event. Only when Russ offered to groom Jelly for free did it hit them.

"You think we should still let her compete?" Andy asked.

Russ nodded. "Why not? It's probably the best therapy for Jelly, after all she's been through. Now, what do you say? Do you want to bring her to my grooming station for a quick cleanup? She's looking a little matted."

"Of course. We really appreciate it."

The Lawsons took off right as Janice and LuAnn arrived with Reena and Richard lagging behind them.

"Did we miss it?" LuAnn asked.

"They found Jelly, and they're getting her cleaned up for the big event."

Everyone began to talk at once, and Tess could hardly make out what any of them were saying.

"This is the best day ever." Reena held her hand to her chest. "Truly."

"Who had her?" Richard asked. "Where was she all this time?"

"With Winston James."

Richard's mouth flew open. "Oh my goodness! Well, I'm not surprised, especially after finding out that he fabricated those stories in the *Canine Companion*."

"I just can't believe he would steal someone else's animal." Reena shook her head. "He seemed like such a nice man."

"Nice man, indeed." LuAnn clucked her tongue.

"Jelly is safe now, and that's what really matters." Reena leaned down to scoop up Beauvine. "Now we can all relax and enjoy this last day together."

"Last day together." Richard spoke the words, and his eyes misted over. "I can't believe we all have to leave tomorrow."

Before Tess could think of anything to say, she noticed Jordan approaching with his wife. He took several steps toward them. "I just heard the news. The police found Jelly?"

"Yes." Tess felt the sting of tears in her eyes. "They found her."

"And *not* on my bus." He laughed.

Tess bowed her head, shame washing over her. "Jordan, I'm so sorry I suspected you. To be honest, I was grasping at straws. I just wanted so badly to find that little doll for those sweet kids. They've missed her so much."

"My feelings aren't hurt. I'm made of tougher stuff than that. And something good came of all that craziness last night. It involves Princess Penelope."

"Princess Penelope?"

He quirked a brow. "The dog you thought I'd stolen."

"Oh, *that* Princess Penelope." Tess felt her cheeks grow warm.

"That police officer brought his mom by this morning, and she fell in love with Penelope. They were a match made in heaven. We signed the adoption papers just now, and that little pooch is headed to her forever home."

"That's great news, Jordan." Tess could hardly believe it, in fact. "What a blissful ending to such a twisted tale. So have you forgiven me for suspecting you?"

"I've forgiven you." His smile faded. "To be honest, the whole thing has really convinced me that I need to be more guarded in my comments about pedigree dogs. I hope you know I'm a dog lover, through and through. Like I said before, I don't discriminate. Even a pedigree dog is okay in my book. They're not responsible for how they came into the world."

"True."

He glanced at his watch. "I would stay and chat, but I'm headed to the warehouse on the back side of the arena. Local animal control officers have called me in to help with a mill dog rescue that took place yesterday. We'll be rehabbing the dogs and then finding homes for them, so I'll be in the area for a while, if you'd like to help."

"I would love that. You work with mill dogs too?"

"I work with all dogs, Tess." He turned to address Reena, a look of pure admiration in his eyes. "Missy and I will be in touch, Reena. We can't thank you enough for all of your help with our organization."

"Of course, Jordan." Reena smiled at him. "I was honored to play a role. I can't wait to see how the documentary turns out. If you need anything, don't hesitate to ask."

Jordan and Missy said their goodbyes and then walked away.

"Could this day get any better?" LuAnn asked. "I'm just giddy that the Lawsons have their dog back."

Janice nodded in agreement. "You really did your legwork on this one, Tess. I'm so proud of you. We all are."

"Winnie gave me the final clue but didn't even realize it. All this time she wanted a good night's sleep, and it was Jelly keeping her awake. That poor little dog was begging for help."

"I'm just glad you figured it out," Reena said. "I think you have a soft spot for dogs after all, don't you, Tess?"

"I guess so." She couldn't help but smile as she thought about it.

Through the ever-growing crowd she caught a glimpse of Geneva racing toward her in that lime-green and hot-pink outfit. The young woman carried a newspaper in her hand. Gigi tagged along on her leash, dressed in her matching getup. "Tess, did you see the paper?" Geneva thrust it in Tess's direction.

"Paper?" She shook her head. "No, I'm sorry. I've been busy."

"She's been helping the police locate the Lawsons' missing dog," Janice explained. "Isn't that wonderful?"

"What?" Geneva reached down to pick up Gigi, who licked her on the cheek. "Really?"

"Yes." Tess nodded. "Russ is grooming her now. She's going to be competing in Best in Show after all."

For a moment, Geneva hesitated. Then she said, "I wish her the best. Gigi and I will be watching from the sidelines." She pointed at the newspaper. "Check out the headlines, Tess. It's all about the raid on the puppy mill. Mr. and Mrs. Matranga have both been taken into custody, and the dogs are all safe, right here in this very building."

"Yes, we just heard." Excitement welled up inside of Tess as she responded. To think, those pups were all safe and sound. "Paws on Wheels is going to help them."

"What great news for those dogs," Janice said. "I pray they all find wonderful forever homes."

"Me too. I was so relieved to read the news," Geneva said. "Those poor puppies deserve a better life. Now they can have it. According to the article the Matrangas will have their day in court soon. Now if you all will excuse me, Gigi and I are headed back to the warehouse. I've volunteered to help out. Doesn't that sound like fun?" She waved and then disappeared into the crowd.

"She's sweet to help," Janice said.

"Very," Tess added. She found herself distracted by Reena, whose jaw was clenched. "You okay over there?"

Reena shook her head. "No. This might be wrong of me, but I hope that judge shows those mill dog owners no mercy at all. They don't deserve it, after all they've put those dogs through."

LuAnn rested her hand on Reena's arm. "You feel very strongly about this, don't you?"

"Well, of course." She paused and appeared to relax a little. "Maybe it's just leftover guilt from my younger years. I used to own expensive poodles. I bought them from a breeder in Lancaster County. I found out, years into it, that the breeder was keeping those sweet mama dogs in awful conditions. But I've never gotten over the guilt of knowing that I actually gave her my money. People like me kept her in business. That's why I agreed to help Jordan, in part to ease my own conscience."

"What's the solution to the puppy mill problem?" Richard asked. "Or is there one?"

"There are some wonderful breeders out there," Reena said. "We just need to encourage all of them to treat their dogs with the care and respect they deserve. Then these pedigreed pups can live long, healthy lives."

"Agreed," Tess said.

"Not everyone can adopt a dog," Reena said. "But we can all do something. We can donate food and dog toys to local shelters, even show up to walk or bathe the dogs. Every little bit helps."

"Great ideas." LuAnn smiled. "We should start a drive to do that."

"Before or after you plan your wedding?" Tess asked. "I'm just curious."

"Oh, right. I am a little busy right now." LuAnn laughed. "But I'm never too busy to pick up dog food for pups in need."

Tess felt her stomach rumble. She glanced around until her gaze landed on the snack bar. "Hey, speaking of food, am I the only one who skipped breakfast this morning? Anyone want to join me for a cup of coffee before the big event?"

All laughter and smiles, they headed to the snack bar to celebrate.

# CHAPTER NINETEEN

*April 12ᵗʰ, 1862*

Despite Prudence's greatest fears, the young soldier had improved. Her prayers, though feeble at times, had not been in vain. She had watched in awe as he grew stronger, day after day. Best of all, she had enjoyed watching the dog, who refused to leave his master's side. It did not go unnoticed that he remained loyal, no matter Nate's condition.

In so many ways, this kindness reminded her of the Lord's love and compassion for her. God would not leave or forsake her, no matter what. Yes, she would go through difficult times, but—like Jack—He would remain faithful. She would never be alone.

On the twelfth of April another Union soldier arrived. He surely came expecting his friend Nate to be at death's door, for the look of shock on his face when he saw the man standing was almost comical.

Prudence watched as Nate crossed the room to greet his comrade.

"William!" He grabbed the young soldier by the shoulders. "So good to see you! What brings you this way?"

"I've—I've come..." the man stammered. "On official business."

"To take Jack home in my stead?" Nate asked. "Did I not say I would do that myself?"

"You did, but..." The man's words faded away. "You are well, then?"

Nate laughed. "As well as can be expected. This fine woman and her husband have been caring for me since I arrived, with the aid of a local doctor. Though, between you and me, I think Prudence has a mite more knowledge than the doctor."

"Thank you for caring for my friend, Prudence." William nodded in her direction.

"I am happy to be of service," she responded.

Nate walked to the window and peered outside. "She's been a godsend. Things looked bleak for a few days there, but the Lord has seen fit to restore me so I can move forward with my task to take Jack home. I plan to leave in the morning, in fact."

"Then I will go with you. I've brought a wagon from our division."

"You've brought a wagon? Why didn't you come on horseback?" Nate asked.

The man paled. "Well, to be perfectly frank, I came with the task of transporting your lifeless body home to your family in New York. I didn't think a horse would do."

"I see." Nate seemed to lose himself to his thoughts for a moment. "Well, if you don't mind, I'd like to wait on that. See, I promised Alex I'd deliver Jack, and I'm a man of my word, so let's hold off on my death for a few more years, shall we?" Nate slung his arm over William's shoulder. "There's much I have yet to do in this life."

"Clearly." William erupted in laughter.

Jack nudged himself between them and jumped up and down, as if to be a part of the action. Prudence watched it all, her heart swelling with joy. Before she could help herself, she knelt down and threw her arms around the dog's neck and planted a kiss on his head.

"For his service," she explained to the soldiers, who looked on with half-smiles. "To thank him."

"I'm sure he's very grateful for your care as well, ma'am." William tipped his hat. "I can't thank you enough for tending to Nate here, and for offering care to Jack on his journey home."

"God has placed me in this very place for this very reason."

"And the people in your care?" he asked.

"Are more precious to me than I could ever say."

# CHAPTER TWENTY

L ook, everyone! Jelly is entering the ring."

"She looks amazing." Janice's eyes widened, and she drew her hands to her chest. "Russ did a fabulous job on her cut."

Tess glanced to her right, where Tandi and her children looked on while Andy led Jelly to the designated spot in the ring. The little doll didn't look any worse for wear. She pranced around like a princess waiting for her subjects to bow in reverence.

The judge started with a gorgeous black-and-tan dachshund, the one who had taken Gigi's place at the last minute. The owner was a handsome young man with dark curls, about Geneva's age.

The judge entered the ring dressed in a fabulous tuxedo. He walked with confidence toward the animals. With a serious expression on his face, he examined the dachshund thoroughly, then made his way to the next dog, a wire-haired terrier. Next came a standard poodle, a majestic thing with the most gorgeous cut Tess had ever seen. After that, the judge moved to a tiny Yorkie, who couldn't stand still, despite his owner's best attempt. From there, the judge walked over to the St. Bernard, a gentle giant named Everest. Next came a gorgeous, beautifully groomed Old English sheepdog. Finally, the judge headed to Angelica, who stood at attention like a soldier awaiting a battle cry.

"She just takes your breath away," Richard said. "What a pro."

After looking over the other dogs in the ring, the judge instructed the owners to run them in a circle.

"Look at Jelly's fur! It looks like velvet." Reena clasped a hand over her mouth and then pulled it away. "Isn't she the most beautiful thing you've ever seen?"

"She is," Tess agreed. "And Russ did a fabulous job of grooming her."

"You won't believe what Russ did." Tandi glanced her way and smiled. "He's offered us a lifetime of grooming for Jelly, absolutely free. Isn't that generous of him? We're so blessed." Her gaze shifted back to the ring.

"What?" Tess could hardly believe her ears. "Really?"

"Yep." Tandi kept her gaze on Angelica. "And it's not contingent upon whether or not she wins today."

"Oh, she'll win," Reena hollered out so loud that several people turned around to look at her. "She's a beauty queen, that one."

They watched as the dogs made their way around the ring. The judge called out several of the dogs to take a second run around the loop—the St. Bernard, the wire-haired terrier, and Jelly. Tess fought the temptation to shout, "Go, Jelly!" as the precious pooch made the circle one last time. Tess held her breath as the announcements were made.

"Best in Show goes to the cocker spaniel, Angelica!" The judge pointed to the beautiful dog, and the audience roared their approval of his decision. Tess's heart soared as she watched Andy lead the winner to the center of the ring.

The celebration carried on until Andy and Jelly finally made their way to the sidelines. At that point, the local media swept in for an interview. Tandi and the kids joined Andy and Jelly, but Tess and the others stayed behind.

When things finally calmed down, Tess walked up to Andy and reached down to pet Jelly's head.

"Great job, Jelly Bean! You were amazing out there."

"She did great, didn't she?" Andy beamed like a proud papa.

"She sure did." LuAnn bent down and gave Jelly a kiss on the head. "She's done Wayfarers Inn proud. She's our first Canine Companion Competition winner!"

"Where are you headed next, Lawson family?" Tess asked. "Is there another competition around the bend?"

"Well, the big national show is coming up in a couple of months." Andy scratched Jelly on the head. "But you know what? We've decided not to compete."

Tess could hardly believe it. "But, why? Jelly's got plenty of years left in her for the competition circuit."

"I know, but we've decided that's not the kind of life we want for her. It's been a fun run, but we're done."

"I think that's a fine decision," Reena said with a smile. "And best of all, Jelly goes out a winner."

"What about you, Richard?" Tess asked. "Will you keep Schmaltzy in the ring?"

He shrugged. "Yes, but I might be a little distracted to think about that for a while."

"Distracted?" Tess and LuAnn asked in unison.

Richard cleared his throat. "I've decided to take a little road trip up to Pittsburgh."

"Why?" LuAnn asked.

"Because a certain lovely lady I know lives there, and I'm hoping she'll show me around."

Reena's cheeks flushed the prettiest color of pink. "I think they were asking you what's coming next with Schmaltzy, not what's coming next with your love life."

He laughed. "Well, with me you get two answers for the price of one. They're linked, you see. As long as there are dogs to show, I'll show them. As long as I've got an opportunity to slip my hand into this pretty lady's, I'll do it."

"Well now." Janice crossed her arms at her chest. "Am I hearing this right?"

"It's better than a scene from a soap opera." Reena giggled. "But at our age I don't think we have time for commercials."

This garnered a laugh from Richard, who ended up in a fit of coughing and sneezing.

"Oh, brother," he said when he finally caught his breath. "I don't know when I've ever laughed as much as I have with you, Reena."

"Hope I don't kill you with my sense of humor. And by the way, you really need to get that upper respiratory stuff checked out, Richard. I've never heard so much sneezing."

He saluted. "Yes, ma'am. As soon as I can, I'll see the doctor." His eyes twinkled. "But I already know what he'll tell me. I'm allergic to dogs, you see."

"What?" Everyone in the room spoke at once.

Tess could hardly believe her ears. "You're allergic?"

"Well, not to all breeds. I do pretty well with schnauzers and poodles. I'm even okay with Maltese and Lhasa apso. Some spaniels don't bother me. But put me in a room with a short-haired hound dog, and I'm a mess."

"How in the world do you make it through the dog show?"

He reached into his pocket and came out with an inhaler. "This, and I'm also on a daily dose of antihistamine. I usually end up doubling that during the show."

That would account for all the sneezing over the last few days.

Tess paused to think through what she'd just learned about the man. "Wow, all I can say is, you must surely love dogs."

"I do, and they're worth a few sneezes and coughs."

"I guess." Tess grew more serious. "As long as you know your limits. I'd hate for you to have a severe reaction."

"I've learned how to live with it and know what to do to keep things under control. No worries."

"But, wait." Reena's face contorted. "Beauvine is a short-haired Chihuahua-dachshund mix. Are you saying you're allergic to him?"

"Yes, but don't fret. I'll up my medication." Richard winked. "It'll be worth it to spend more time with you, Reena."

"That might be the sweetest thing I've ever heard a man say." Reena's face lit into the prettiest smile.

"Or the most dangerous," LuAnn whispered in Tess's ear. "I hope this relationship doesn't destroy the man's health. He's not exactly a spring chicken."

"Oh, I don't know about that. He's looks pretty young and carefree right now," Tess whispered back. "Besides, none of us are spring chickens. Remember when we thought sixty was old?"

"Let's change the conversation, shall we?" LuAnn laughed.

Tess shifted her attention back to Reena, whose cheeks flushed pink as Richard slipped his arm over her shoulder. He leaned over and gave her a tiny kiss on the cheek.

Well, if that didn't beat everything. These two really were the perfect match. When Reena Newberry made up her mind about something, she went after it—whether it was a dog or a man.

Richard took Reena by the arm, and they disappeared into the crowd.

"Now that's true love," LuAnn said. "A man who's willing to risk his life to be with the woman he loves? Priceless."

"I'm not altogether sure his doctor would agree it's the wisest choice, but who am I to say?" Tess laughed.

She caught a glimpse of Geneva pushing through the crowd in their direction.

"I can't believe I missed it. Did Jelly win?"

"Yes."

"That's wonderful."

Tess couldn't help but notice that Geneva looked genuinely happy about that news.

Geneva scooped Gigi into her arms. "We had the best time back there. I got to know the little doggies. So many of them need serious help, but others are in pretty good shape. Oh, and I met that Jordan guy, the one who runs the Paws on Wheels organization. His wife Missy is great. We really hit it off."

"I'm so glad," Tess said. "So, are you and Gigi bowing out of future competitions?"

"Yes. I called the director this morning and told him everything. He agreed with you, that I could have her DNA tested, but I don't think I want to go that route."

"Even though Gigi's grandpa is now in custody?" LuAnn asked.

Geneva wrinkled her nose. "I hadn't thought about that, but I still don't think I'll go for it. I'm perfectly happy with my little girl, just as she is. I'll miss the AKC events, but there are other ways to socialize. Until then..." She nuzzled Gigi closer. "I'll go on loving my baby girl, papers or no papers."

"Attagirl."

"And"—Geneva winked—"I have news."

"Oh, what's that?"

"I'm getting another dog!"

"Really? What kind?"

"He's one of the mill dogs, a hodgepodge of several breeds. I can't even imagine what his DNA would look like, but he's adorable—part hound dog and part English springer spaniel, I think." She giggled. "I'm really not sure."

"Not a purebred, then?"

"Purebred, schmur-bred." Geneva laughed. "He's the funniest looking little thing—one ear stands up and the other one kind of flops over. I looked down in that pen and saw that little angel, and my heart just flipped!" She clasped her hands together and sighed. "I wasn't sure Gigi would be willing to share me with anyone else, but they're like two peas in a pod. You should see them together! They just played and played."

"A dachshund and an English springer hound." Tess laughed at the image that presented.

"Yes." She giggled. "But don't worry. They won't be having any puppies. She put her hand up, as if taking a pledge. "I'm a responsible pet owner."

"You seem like a very responsible pet owner, Geneva. And I've never met anyone who adores her dog the way you do."

"Some would just say I'm weird."

With the wave of a hand, Tess attempted to dismiss that concern. "Well, let them say what they like."

"I've kind of gotten used to seeing you and Gigi dress alike," Janice chimed in. "Every morning I look forward to seeing what the two of you are wearing."

"Thank you." Geneva shrugged. "Oh, I almost forgot to tell you something. I've had the most marvelous idea."

"What's that?"

"I'm thinking about setting up a booth at the next dog show to sell my designs."

"I think that's the perfect solution. And you can use Gigi and your new baby as models."

"Yes, my thoughts exactly. If anyone asks why Gigi's not competing anymore, I'll just tell them she's retired so that she can walk the runway."

"Perfect."

"It's going to be tough to get started, but I think I can do it. After talking to Emma, my imagination just took off. Before long, I was sketching ideas right and left." Her eyes sparkled. "I'm not upset about Gigi anymore. I mean, who cares if she can compete or not? Showing off my creations at the show was half the fun. She reached to squeeze Tess's hand. "Have I told you how grateful I am for your encouragement? I might have left this competition completely devastated if it hadn't been for you."

"Really?"

"Yes. I just needed to redirect my thinking."

"Well, don't thank me. Thank Him." Tess pointed upward. "All the best ideas come from Him."

"You think God really cares about me?"

Tess blinked. "Well, of course He does. And He cares about Gigi too."

"How could anyone not love Gigi? She's my little baby. Sometimes I think our dogs are the only ones who will ever truly love us for who we are." Tears sprang to cover her lashes.

"Hey, I'm not so sure I would agree with that." Tess gestured with her head. "The owner of that black-and-tan dachsie has been looking this way ever since you walked up. He's a real cutie."

"What?" Her cheeks flamed pink. "You think?"

"I know." Tess looked over her shoulder and caught another glimpse of the young man staring at Geneva and Gigi. "So, never say never—that's all."

"Well, I should probably put out a 'Must Love Dogs' shingle on my apartment door. Any guy who gets me gets a package deal."

"There are a lot of dog lovers out there, so I wouldn't worry too much about that. In the meantime, he's walking this way. I think he wants to chat."

"Oh my goodness." Her cheeks flushed, but she worked up the courage to take a few steps in his direction.

"Well, what do you think of that?" LuAnn asked. "God works in mysterious ways."

"He does, indeed," Janice added.

Tess couldn't help but smile as she looked at her friends. "He really does. And this week He's used dogs—mutts and purebreds alike—to teach me a few lessons."

"Like what?" Janice asked.

"It doesn't matter where we've come from or what our heritage might be. He can still use us in mighty ways."

"Amen, sister." LuAnn patted her on the back. "I'm glad to have you on board the dog train."

"I think I've always been on board. I just needed to see things through their eyes for a while." Tess paused. "I've been thinking, the 103rd Division had their mascot, Jack. In a way, we've got our own mascots here at Wayfarers—Huck and Tom."

"True," LuAnn agreed. "They're already on the job, lifting morale."

"They are, indeed."

Tess's heart swelled with joy as she thought about how God had blessed them with such precious pets. Suddenly, she could hardly wait to get home to show them just how loved they were.

Dear Reader,

Those who know me well know what a dog lover I am. I simply can't get enough of those adorable four-legged friends. In my own personal journey, my dogs have been a comfort in times of deep grief and a help in times of trouble. (You might not believe me if I told you that my dachshund, Copper, alerted me to the fact that I had squamous cell skin cancer several years ago, but it's true!)

I've been fascinated with the topic of dog rescue for some time, which was why I added the Paws on Wheels story to this tale (er, *tail?*). I love pedigree dogs and have no issues with responsible breeders, but most of my babies have been rescues. That's why I wanted to mix it up in this story—celebrating dogs of every make and model. If you met my crazy little chiweeniee, Annie, you would quickly learn that she's a lot like her owner, hyper and loud. And if you met my newest shepherd-mix puppy, Bella, you would discover that I stink at fostering. I want to keep those babies—forever.

I could think of no finer conundrum for Tess, LuAnn, and Janice than to drop several dogs into Wayfarers Inn at once. This, of course, presented a problem, because the inn had never allowed dogs as guests before. As I talked through the story concept with my editors at Guideposts, they saw the benefit of a "trial run" while the dog show is in town.

Some time ago I got to know a little dog named Jax—a dachshund/terrier mix from our local shelter. His journey began in Texas, where he landed in the shelter shortly after

Hurricane Harvey. Jax was transported north to Connecticut, where he now lives a happy, fulfilling life with a ten-year-old boy as his best friend. His story was another reason to add the Paws on Wheels angle to this story. (Side note: I love looking at pictures of Jax playing in the snow. Can you imagine leaving hot, humid Texas to live in snowy Connecticut?)

I would like to share one last dog-related story. While writing this book, I came across a tiny short-haired red dachshund at our local shelter. She was sixteen-years old, blind, and had cancer. I found her shivering in a crate, lying in her own urine. I knew she had to be mine. I took that little doll home and named her Gigi, after the Gigi in this story. She wasn't long for this world—she was battling an upper respiratory infection she'd picked up at the shelter—but she was loved until the very last minute of her life. I mention Gigi's story, in part, because the day I picked her up from the shelter, there were 711 dogs and cats looking for homes. That same day the shelter took in another 68 animals. If you're looking for a pet, please consider adopting one from your local shelter.

Thanks for reading, y'all!
Janice Thompson

# ABOUT THE AUTHOR

A ward-winning author Janice Thompson got her start in the industry writing screenplays and musical comedies for the stage. Janice has published over 110 books for the Christian market, crossing genre lines to write cozy mysteries, historicals, romances, nonfiction books, devotionals, children's books, and more. She particularly enjoys writing lighthearted, comedic tales because she enjoys making readers laugh.

Janice is passionate about her faith and does all she can to share the joy of the Lord with others, which is why she particularly enjoys writing. Her tagline, "Love, Laughter, and Happily Ever Afters!" sums up her take on life.

She lives in Spring, Texas, where she leads a rich life with her family, a host of writing friends, and three mischievous dogs, Annie, Bella, and Copper. When she's not busy writing or playing with her nine grandchildren, Janice can be found in the kitchen, baking specialty cakes and cookies for friends and loved ones. No matter what she's cooking up—books, cakes, cookies, or mischief—she does her best to keep the Lord at the center of it all.

# CANINE WAR MASCOTS

For as long as there have been wars, there have been war dogs like Jack. In fact, if you research Civil War dogs you will find that many, particularly mascots, were loyal, dedicated members of their companies, battalions, or regiments. They marched with their troops, accompanied them into battle, and lifted the morale of all they served alongside.

The real-life Jack was made famous when his story was told in *Harper's Weekly* in 1862. His original owner was a Confederate jailer in Virginia, but when a group of Union soldiers was taken captive in Virginia, Jack fell in line with them. He followed the Union officers to their war camp in North Carolina and remained a loyal fixture.

Jack was described as gentle and timid when with his friends but ferocious when those he loved were crossed. He learned the various roll calls and lined up with his troops, taking his place by the drummer. As for whether or not he preferred the Union politics to those of the South, one cannot be sure. No doubt his kind treatment by Union soldiers endeared them to him and won his heart.

To learn more about Jack, go to: americacomesalive.com/ 2014/07/14/dog-jack-mascot-volunteer-union/.

# Pup-Cakes

### Cake Ingredients

1 box white cake mix

1 cup water

3 eggs

½ cup vegetable oil

½ cup mini chocolate
chips

1 tablespoon flour
(for coating chocolate
chips)

### Frosting Ingredients

2 sticks butter (room
temperature)

1 cup Crisco (white)

1 teaspoon vanilla extract

½ teaspoon almond extract

1 bag (7–8 cups)
confectioners sugar

1–2 tablespoons milk
(as needed to thin)

### Decorating Tools/Needs

1 12" piping bag

Wilton grass tip (#233 or
similar) with coupler

½ cup (regular sized)
chocolate chips

5 pink Starburst candies
(slightly softened)

**Instructions**

Cupcakes: Combine the first four ingredients and mix well. Place chocolate chips and flour in a (separate) small bowl and stir with a spoon until chips are lightly covered in flour. Add floured chips to the cake batter and gently mix. Scoop batter with an ice cream scoop into lined cupcake tins and bake at 350 degrees for approximately 15 minutes or until they spring back to the touch.

Frosting: Cream butter, Crisco, and extracts in mixing bowl until light and fluffy. Turn mixer to lowest speed and slowly add confectioners sugar and milk. If necessary, add additional confectioners sugar or milk until the frosting is fluffy but holds its shape.

To decorate: Prepare icing bag by attaching the coupler and tip, then fill with white frosting. Pipe "fur" onto the cupcakes to look like a puppy, (longer on the sides for ears). Then add upside-down chocolate chips for eyes and nose. If you like, you can make a little pink tongue using slightly softened pink Starburst candy.

Read on for a sneak peek of another exciting book
in the Secrets of Wayfarers Inn series!

# SPECIAL DELIVERY
## by Kathleen Y'Barbo

It was a beautiful wedding on an absolutely perfect day in
May. Janice Eastman stood outside Christ Fellowship Church
and dabbed at her eyes with one hand while waving to the happy
couple with the other. Her daughter, Stacy, a bridesmaid, leaned
against her.

"Can you believe it, Mom? Our Stuart is married."

"It's wonderful," she said.

"It is." Stacy glanced around and then let out a long breath.
"Have you seen Larry? He's disappeared again."

Stacy's six-year-old son was prone to wandering, not out of
spite or disobedience but rather out of curiosity. Unfortunately,
sometimes his curiosity got him in trouble.

"I haven't seen him since he carried the ring down the aisle
and then sat by me through the service. When we all stood up
to leave, I assumed he was behind me."

Stacy gave Janice a look and then immediately formed a
smile. "It's Stuart's big day. I'll go hunt for Larry. He's probably
with Dash. You'd best get to the reception."

Janice's phone chirped in the pocket of her coat, but she ignored it. As mother of the groom, substitute mother of the bride, and brand-new grandmother to the bride's grown daughter who served as maid of honor, she did not want to miss a moment of this.

Dr. Stuart Eastman helped his bride, Zelda, into the vintage white convertible the couple had rented for the occasion and then hurried around to the other side. Just before he climbed in, he found Janice in the crowd and waved.

"We finally did it, Ma. How about that?"

"How about that indeed," Janice called with a grin. "Your father would be so proud."

And he certainly would have. Even now as she stood on the steps of the church her late husband, Lawrence, had pastored for so long, Janice could feel her husband beaming with joy. When she first lost him to an automobile accident on a snowy day not so many years ago, she had taken up the habit of speaking to him in the dark hours of the night as if he were there.

She rarely did that anymore, but she did so now, casting a quick glance heavenward to whisper, "I wish you were here to see this, Lawrence."

Two sets of arms went around her, one belonging to LuAnn Sherill and the other to Tess Wallace. Together they formed the Inn Crowd, best friends for life and innkeepers at Marietta's historic Wayfarers Inn.

"What a beautiful couple," Tess said. "I'm thrilled for them."

"From the flowers to the music to the sunshine when the forecasters predicted rain, everything was just perfect," LuAnn proclaimed. "And Zelda is absolutely radiant."

Janice managed a nod as tears once again flowed. "I swore I wouldn't cry," she said as she took Tess's offer of a handkerchief and dabbed at her eyes. "But here I am doing exactly what I said I wouldn't. I've got to fix my face so I don't look ridiculous in the reception pictures."

"Oh honey," Tess said gently. "We all waited a long time and prayed a lot of prayers to see that son of yours married. Not only did you gain a daughter-in-law, but you also got a granddaughter. Those are happy tears. And you're next, LuAnn. We'll need buckets of tissues to get through your wedding. I'm sure of it."

Janice's phone chirped again, a reminder that she had not yet listened to her phone message. She frowned and reached into her pocket.

"Something wrong?" LuAnn asked.

"No, it's just that someone phoned during the ceremony, and the caller left a message. Stuart set up my phone, and I have no idea how to keep it from beeping until I listen to my messages. It's driving me crazy."

"Maybe you should just listen to it," LuAnn offered.

"Yes, I think I will." Janice waved goodbye to the newlyweds as the car pulled away from the curb and headed toward the reception venue. She returned her attention to the phone and pressed the button to play her messages.

"Mrs. Eastman," the caller began, "this is Dr. Amanda Weaver. I'm sorry to be calling on a Saturday, but I'm here catching up on work and saw that your mammogram results are in. I'm sorry to tell you this, but..."

Janice fumbled with her phone, and it might have landed on the steps had Tess not jumped in to grab it. "Thank you," she managed as she tucked the phone back into her pocket, her mind reeling.

"What in the world is wrong with you?" Tess demanded. "Did something happen?"

"Nothing," she said and then instantly regretted the deception. "Yes there is something, but I don't want to talk about it. Not here and certainly not now. Wait until we are at the inn after the reception. It is absolutely nothing worth bothering about at my son's wedding reception."

"You're sure?" LuAnn asked, concern etching her expression.

"I'm certain." Janice forced a smile. "Now let's get over to the reception. I'm under strict instructions not to tarry, because there will be photographs taken there before the food is served."

Several hours later, the bride and groom headed off to the airport to begin their tropical honeymoon. Janice and her friends returned to the inn and kicked off their shoes in their suite of rooms on the top floor of the inn.

"All right," Tess said as she set a tea tray in front of them. "I think we all agree that was an absolutely perfect wedding and reception."

"It was," LuAnn said. "The food was divine. I got the caterer's card just in case we need someone in a pinch. She really had such a beautiful way of styling her food."

"And that venue," Tess said. "I'll be honest and admit I was a little bothered by the fact that they didn't choose the inn, but now that I see how many people they had attending, I realize we could never have fit them all here."

Janice poured steaming water over her Earl Grey teabag and listened to LuAnn and Tess discuss the details of the wedding. She knew what they were doing, but she let them fill the silence with this welcome distraction for a few more minutes.

Then, finally, she retrieved her phone from her pocket. Instantly both women fell silent.

"I'm just going to play the message first, and then we can discuss it. All right?"

"Sure," Tess said, while LuAnn nodded in agreement.

"Mrs. Eastman," the message began, "this is Dr. Amanda Weaver. I'm sorry to be calling on a Saturday, but I'm here catching up on work and saw that your mammogram results are in. I'm sorry to tell you this, but you're going to need further testing to be certain of what we're looking at. I wish I could tell you more on the phone, but you'll need to speak to me in person on Monday. Please call the office when you can. I'll leave a note with the staff to let them know you'll need to be put directly through to me."

The call ended, and the room went silent. Janice tucked the phone back into her pocket. "Well," she said as brightly as she could manage, "that's it. That was the message I listened to outside the church."

There. The news she'd been holding inside her all during the reception was out. Spoken. Her friends' expressions mirrored how she felt.

"It's going to be fine," she managed.

"Of course it is," LuAnn agreed.

"Yes," Tess added. "You've got the best doctor, and there was nothing in that message that sounded like she is worried."

"I'm sure you're right," Janice said. "But after losing my mother and my aunt…" She paused. "No. There is nothing to be afraid of. This did not take the Lord by surprise even if it surprised me. No matter what comes of this, He will take care of me."

Janice knew this deep in her heart. These were words she'd said to so many others in her position as a pastor's wife, and she had seen God do exactly that.

It *would* be fine. God *would* take care of her.

"Of course He will," LuAnn said. "There's no question of that."

Tess shook her head. "None at all, but the question for now is how can LuAnn and I help you through this?"

Oh how she hated the idea that there was anything to get through. Instead of responding with the words she wanted to say, she gave her answer a moment's thought.

"For today there really isn't anything to help me through. The message was fairly vague, so let's just see what this is all about on Monday. In the meantime, I am not going to let this ruin the rest of my weekend."

"Yes, of course," Tess said. "Dwelling on this won't make anything clearer or cause Monday to come any sooner."

"Well, no," LuAnn said. "But talking about it might help if you're feeling worried."

"Thank you, but there really isn't anything to talk about until we know if there is actually a problem. In the meantime, I'm fine."

"Janice is right," Tess said. "Most of the time these things turn out to be nothing."

"Yes, I was just reading an article about that recently," LuAnn said. "Our technology has gotten so sensitive that the tests are showing far too many false positives. I'll bet that's exactly what happened here."

What was wrong with her? Had the situation been different and Tess or LuAnn was the one who'd gotten that phone call, she would have been saying exactly the same things. Yet hearing them now did not help at all, despite the fact that she understood her friends were trying desperately to find the right words to lift her mood and take away her fears.

"Thank you, ladies. You're the best friends a girl could have." She stifled a yawn. "But as much as I would like to stay up and chat, I am absolutely exhausted. I think I'll go to bed."

"We've all had a long day," Tess said. "My pillow is sounding like heaven right now. And we've got a busy week ahead."

LuAnn stifled a yawn. "Oh, that's right. We've got that book convention coming in on Monday."

"Followed by several others in the weeks after. We're at full capacity for the month, and if I think about how busy we will be, I get hives. So I don't think that far ahead." Tess shrugged. "Janice, would you mind if we prayed for you first?"

"Of course not," she said. "I would love that."

Tess started out the prayer, and then LuAnn took up where she left off. Finally it was Janice's turn.

"Thank You, Lord, for Your mercies, for Your assurance of heaven, and for good friends. May I recall all of these things as I walk through whatever You have for me in the coming days."

They all said, "Amen."

With a smile on her face, Janice took her teacup and saucer to the sink in the kitchenette and then bid her best friends good night. After going through her usual nighttime routine, she turned off the lights and settled beneath the covers.

Then, very quietly, Janice fell apart.

# A Note from the Editors

We hope you enjoy Secrets of Wayfarers Inn, created by the Books and Inspirational Media Division of Guideposts, a nonprofit organization that touches millions of lives every day through products and services that inspire, encourage, help you grow in your faith, and celebrate God's love in every aspect of your daily life.

Thank you for making a difference with your purchase of this book, which helps fund our many outreach programs to military personnel, prisons, hospitals, nursing homes, and educational institutions. To learn more, visit Guideposts Foundation.org.

We also maintain many useful and uplifting online resources. Visit Guideposts.org to read true stories of hope and inspiration, access OurPrayer network, sign up for free newsletters, download free e-books, join our Facebook community, and follow our stimulating blogs.

To learn about other Guideposts publications, including the best-selling devotional *Daily Guideposts*, go to ShopGuideposts .org, call (800) 932-2145, or write to Guideposts, PO Box 5815, Harlan, Iowa 51593.

# Sign up for the
# Guideposts Fiction Newsletter
## *and stay up to date on the books you love!*

You'll get sneak peeks of new releases, recommendations from other Guideposts readers, and special offers just for you . . .
## *and it's FREE!*

## Just go to Guideposts.org/Newsletters today to sign up.

# Guideposts.®

### Visit Guideposts.org/Shop
### or call (800) 932-2145

# Find more inspiring fiction in these best-loved Guideposts series!

## *Tearoom Mysteries Series*

Mix one stately Victorian home, a charming lakeside town in Maine, and two adventurous cousins with a passion for tea and hospitality. Add a large scoop of intriguing mystery and sprinkle generously with faith, family, and friends, and you have the recipe for *Tearoom Mysteries.*

## *Sugarcreek Amish Mysteries*

Be intrigued by the suspense and joyful "aha" moments in these delightful stories. Each book in the series brings together two women of vastly different backgrounds and traditions, who realize there's much more to the "simple life" than meets the eye.

## *Mysteries of Martha's Vineyard*

What does Priscilla Latham Grant, a Kansas farm girl know about hidden treasure and rising tides, maritime history and local isle lore? Not much—but to save her lighthouse and family reputation, she better learn quickly!

## *Mysteries of Silver Peak*

Escape to the historic mining town of Silver Peak, Colorado, and discover how one woman's love of antiques helps her solve mysteries buried deep in the town's checkered past.

### To learn more about these books,
### visit Guideposts.org/Shop